So Shall You Reap

ISBN-13: 978-0-9846347-5-0
ISBN-10: 0-9846347-5-4

First printing: August, 2011

Cover design by ThomasMax

Published by:

ThomasMax Publishing
P.O. Box 250054
Atlanta, GA 30325
www.thomasmax.com

So Shall You Reap

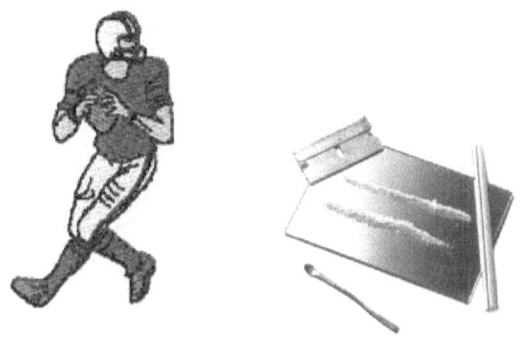

By John House

ThomasMax

Your Publisher
For The 21st Century

Acknowledgments

This is my first published novel, and while no one writes a book for you (unless you're a celebrity whose name guarantees a million seller, in which case the publisher assigns you a ghost writer), I would like to acknowledge:

** Emily Carmain for her encouragement and for keeping me on track with Point of View.

** My friends at Southeastern Writers Association. Learning the craft of writing is continuous and enjoyable when you are around writer friends.

-- John House

To my wife, Pamela, my greatest fan. She makes the low points more bearable and the high points even better

PROLOGUE

A green utility truck bounced over a washboard dirt road, one of its two occupants grimacing from the bone-jarring ride. The narrow road sliced through thick vegetation over a succession of mountain tops where intermittent breaks in the forest revealed vistas of lush green hillsides and fog-shrouded valleys.

Doctor James Smith, an American physician visiting from Georgia, sat in the passenger seat. He turned away from the view and spoke to his driver. "Your country is beautiful but rugged, Pedro."

"Yes, señor. Colombia shows many faces. We are getting near the village."

Three hours into the trip Pedro slowed the vehicle, and plunged it into a thicket of plants. The truck plowed through the vegetation for several minutes before breaking out into a small clearing. Scattered about were five shacks built of rough-hewn planks and tin. Smith saw several dilapidated trucks parked near the crude dwellings. Isolated from the shacks some fifty yards away stood a pen built of chicken wire, reinforced with vertical slats of wood.

Smith's stomach contracted in revulsion to a nauseating odor permeating the air. His companion appeared oblivious to the smell.

Pedro climbed out of the truck, motioning with his upraised hand for his passenger to remain.

Smith glanced at his watch, calculating the time traveled since daybreak. If the anticipated meeting was lengthy, darkness would overtake them on the drive back to the hotel in Bogota.

A commotion at one of the buildings interrupted his thoughts. A door banged outwards, thrown open by two burly dark-skinned men. Their bulging chest muscles and tree-like arms identified them as enforcers. Between them was a screaming Caucasian male who was dragged from the building and thrown to the ground. The man attempted to crawl away from his captors but the larger of the two men grabbed the hapless victim, lifting him by one leg. The enforcers burst out in devilish laughter, swinging the terrified man between them.

Smith watched in morbid curiosity until his attention was diverted to a tall swarthy figure standing alone on the porch. *Ramon Ortega.* The man Smith came here to see.

Several months earlier at a medical conference in Atlanta, Smith, dissatisfied with insurance payment cutbacks and his shrinking income, had voiced his negative opinion of large insurance corporations and government health plans. That vocal seed had eventually led to this meeting with Ortega, a lieutenant to one of the biggest drug cartel leaders in Colombia.

Smith watched Ramon Ortega retrieve a long cylinder from inside his jacket pocket. He extracted a cigar, removed a small tool from a side pocket, clipped the end of the cigar and lit it. Puffing with zeal, he nodded to the enforcers.

The men hoisted the struggling man over their heads, ambled to the pen and threw him into the wire-enclosed area.

The horrific screams from the victim were matched in volume by high-pitched squeals and grunts that increased, while the human sounds lessened until they ceased.

Ortega's expression remained matter of fact. He took a heavy draw on the cigar, and blew smoke rings toward the pen. He gave a hand signal to Pedro, and walked back into the building.

Pedro ran to the passenger door of the truck. He tapped Smith on the shoulder. "Señor Ortega will see you."

CHAPTER 1

Four years later.

Soft light from a full October moon draped over two nude people. They stood waist deep in the cool waters of Lake Oconee, a popular recreational site near Athens, the home of the University of Georgia.

A small-breasted girl, her legs wrapped around the waist of her tall male companion, moaned in animal arousal enhanced by her drug-induced trance. Her partner matched her excitement, their combined movements frantic and rhythmic, ascending to a carnal peak. They broke apart when a high scream echoed across the water from their campsite.

Eddie and Lisa splashed through the water to the bank and raced across the grassy slope to the small bonfire shared with their friends.

Maria, a chubby Hispanic girl, stared up at them, her eyes wide as she pointed to her companion. On the ground a slightly built, fair skinned boy writhed in agony, with thin legs rigidly extended. His head jerked backwards, displaying a mask of fear as he clawed at his throat.

Lisa drew back, shaking, and buried her face in Eddie's chest. "What's wrong with Timmy?"

Timmy's back arched, his head striking the ground with a dull thud. His eyes turned upwards in their orbits, with the white of the globes revealed. His nostrils flared and bloody spittle oozed from the corners of his mouth.

Maria lunged toward him, pushing aside his thrashing arms; she pulled his head to her chest, stroking his face with a gentle touch. She leaned forward to kiss his blue lips but was repulsed when he retched, spewing vomit all over her. The projectile heaving continued, accompanied by rapid jerking motions of his legs, the heels digging small trenches in the soft soil.

The jerking stopped. The flaccid body collapsed to the ground, the head lolling to the left, vomit running down the face and neck.

Eddie recovered from his initial shock and slid across the ground to help his friend. He grabbed Timmy's shoulders to turn him on his side, but a putrid stench from Timmy's relaxed bowel and bladder drove him back. "Damn. What the fuck is happening to him?"

Tears created black rivulets on Maria's cheeks from her smeared mascara. Oblivious to the powerful odor, she cradled her lover's head in her lap, pleading with him to wake up. "You'll be okay, Timmy. We're all here with you. You'll be okay."

Lisa dropped her hands from her face and tugged on Eddie's arm as she stared at Timmy. "I think he had a seizure. I saw my cousin have one several years ago. She had epilepsy and I remember her mouth being bloody because she bit her tongue."

Eddie mustered the courage to move beside Timmy once again. He attempted to open Timmy's mouth but the tightly clenched jaws made it impossible. Uncertain what to do, he turned to Maria and Lisa, but their blank stares offered no help.

The moment of indecision was shattered when Timmy's body arched off the ground, supported by his head in Maria's lap and his heels pressed into the soft dirt. His back remained bowed for a full minute before it collapsed.

The second seizure stirred Eddie to action. He grabbed towels, ran to the lake and plunged them beneath the surface. Another scream cut through the night, like a scalpel through soft flesh. Through Maria's shrieks, Eddie heard Lisa's voice yelling for help as he ran back to them.

Maria, hysterical, rocked back and forth with Timmy's head still in her lap. Her tears fell like black raindrops on his pallid face.

Lisa spun toward Eddie. "He's not breathing!"

CHAPTER 2

It was fourth and goal. Five points down to the Tennessee Volunteers, the ninth ranked NCAA team in the nation.

The loyal fans at Sanford Stadium were on their feet, roaring their support for the University of Georgia Bulldogs who were three feet away from a winning touchdown. Eight seconds remained in the game and Georgia took their last timeout. Score a touchdown and the Bulldogs' second-place ranking in the Bowl Championship Series would be secure. Failure would drop them in the national ranks, dampening their chances for consideration by the Bowl Selection Committee for a major bowl.

Joshua Smith returned to the huddle after a hurried conference with the coach on the sideline. The elusive dream of a NCAA Championship hung on the success of the next play. The tension in the huddle was almost palpable as he relayed the play selected by the offensive coordinator. He wiped his sweaty palms on the small towel tucked in the waistband of his pants and followed his teammates to the line of scrimmage. He stood erect, surveying the defensive setup, his mouth so dry he was concerned he would not be able to call out the signals.

He took his position behind the center, saw his wide receivers could not hear his cadence and backed away. He raised his hands, palms down, and the noise level in the stadium dropped. He said a silent prayer of thanks that the team was not in the visitors' end of the stadium. He looked over the defense again, recognizing the stacked alignment in the center, a formation studied many times on game films.

He straightened up, noting the time remaining on the play clock. He turned left and right, shouting out the signals to check off the called play. He motioned for the tailback to move to a position behind the guard. He repositioned his hands underneath the center and began calling the cadence.

The ball was snapped and the fullback crashed forward. Joshua placed the ball in the player's midsection and with a smooth motion, pulled it back. The opposing linebackers reacted to the fake and jammed the middle of the line. The large bodies of the offensive and defensive linemen formed a wall of sweaty, grunting meat, crashing together, the cleats of their shoes seeking purchase in the dirt to move their opponent. A teeth-jarring collision of the fullback and the onrushing linebackers compounded the mayhem.

Joshua tucked the ball under his right arm, running to his left. His vision played over the field in front, and he saw the right cornerback was not fooled by the play action to the fullback. Joshua realized the balance of the season rested with him. The most important play so far this season and he had checked off the coordinator's call, convinced the cornerback would be suckered in by the fake.

He sprinted toward the sideline, options racing through his mind. He pump-faked toward the center of the field, and rejoiced when the cornerback veered toward the tight end, slanting across the middle. Joshua pulled the ball down, switched it to his left hand and secured it against his side. His entire field of vision narrowed to the orange pylon at the corner of the end zone. His heart pounded as he drove his legs and leaned his body toward the goal.

From the corner of his eye he saw the cornerback recover from the fake pass, aiming for a collision at the one-yard line.

CHAPTER 3

With an agonized cry, Eddie threw himself onto his friend's body. He placed his lips over Timmy's and pinched the nostrils, ignoring the foul-smelling vomit and bloody mucus. After several breaths he started arm thrusts on the scrawny chest, mimicking instructions taught in health class at school.

He wrestled Timmy's head away from Maria and placed him flat on the ground. Eddie worked at a feverish pace to restore life to the cool, limp body. He continued without letup even when his arms ached and his lungs burned with a pain never before experienced.

"God help me," he cried out. His feeling of futility triggered a rational thought and he yelled to Lisa. "Find Timmy's cell phone and call 911."

She scrambled to her feet and ran to the Jeep, ignoring the pain in her bare feet from the sticks, rocks and pine cones in her path.

Eddie returned his attention to Timmy and shouted to Maria, "Help me. Do mouth-to-mouth while I do the chest compressions."

Maria pushed her damp long hair back from her face. She placed her lips over Timmy's mouth, blew hard into it and watched out of the corner of her eye as Eddie performed the chest compressions. She tried to time her efforts to occur between the compressions and they both worked frantically.

Several long minutes later, Eddie became aware of gut-wrenching sobs from Maria and Lisa. He looked up into Lisa's panic-stricken face as she struck her head with her clenched fist.

"I couldn't find the phone," she said. "I'm so sorry, I couldn't find it."

Eddie's resolve collapsed. He grabbed Timmy's hair, pulling the other boy's face to his own. Tears flowed down his cheeks while he rocked back and forth, caressing his friend's cold face. "Damn, Timmy. What did you do? What did you take? Why did you always have to push things?"

He clung to Timmy until he felt a hand on his shoulder. He looked up at Maria, her beautiful face distorted with pain and grief. He gently placed his friend's head on the ground. He leaned forward, clutching his own head between his arms, and sobs racked his body. Several minutes passed before he was aware that Maria and Lisa were beside him, their arms embracing him.

The tears lessened and Eddie, accepting reality, turned to the girls. "Get dressed. I'll go up to the Jeep and find the cell phone. I know it has Joshua's number on speed dial. The game should be over by now, but if he doesn't answer, I'll leave a text message and we'll wait for him to call back. It kills me to realize if we had stayed at the game, Timmy would still be alive."

Lisa threw her arms around Eddie. "Are you going to call the police? I'm so scared. I don't want to go to jail."

"There's no way out for us. We're not going to leave Timmy here," he said. "Whatever they do to us will be minor compared to what has happened to Timmy. Don't worry, I won't call them yet. I'll wait until I hear from Joshua and I'll ask him what I should do."

Maria kissed Timmy's lifeless lips and placed his head on the jacket Eddie had folded and given to her. She stood up slowly. "What will happen to us?"

Eddie embraced both girls, squeezing them against his own trembling body. His eyes remained focused on the only true friend he had ever known. "I don't have any idea but at the moment, I don't even care."

CHAPTER 4

Joshua stopped his fall with his outstretched right arm. He spun again, shaking loose from the safety that had joined the pursuit. Somehow Joshua regained his balance and he launched his body toward the goal line, extending the ball cradled in both hands across the imaginary plane above the chalk line. Even before he hit the ground the tremendous roar in the stadium announced his success.

He soon found himself at the bottom of a pile of ecstatic teammates and he relished the moment, one of the happiest times of his life. When he was able to pull away from all the back pounding and hugs, he jogged off the field, giving way to the special team players who would attempt the unneeded extra point.

At the sideline the offensive coordinator met him. Joshua felt a slap against his helmet and heard the words whispered in his ear. "Good thing you got across that goal line."

The locker room was clear of players and reporters. The frenzy surrounding the win was gone and Joshua, now showered and in his street clothes, sat stunned on a bench in front of his locker. The text message on his cell phone had shattered the joy present minutes before, replacing it with a pain that squeezed his heart like a vise. The iron will and confidence he experienced earlier in the game had vanished, and he felt helpless and hopeless.

His brother was dead and he, Joshua, would have to face his parents awaiting him somewhere outside the victors' locker room. A heavy burden had been thrust upon him and he wasn't sure he could handle it.

He hit the speed dial on his cellular phone for Pamela Jane Holmes—his fiancée, PJ—and typed in a brief text message to meet him at his Jeep. He couldn't face his parents, at least not until he was able to confirm Timmy's death. Joshua trembled and rubbed a hand across his forehead. His life would never be the same again.

CHAPTER 5

The light from the full moon played hide and seek behind gathering clouds, casting shadows as it filtered through the tall Georgia pines.

Joshua felt PJ squeeze his right arm, a reminder she was still there. He hadn't spoken a word for the past ten minutes.

"What are you thinking about so hard?" she asked.

Joshua maintained his focus on the road ahead. "I'm sorry I tuned you out. It wasn't my intention. I'm just wondering if I did the right thing in dodging my parents. I know I can say I'm doing it for their sake, but that's a bunch of crap and we both know it. I didn't have the guts to face them together. Mom would be hysterical and my father would immediately take charge and start calling in favors from his friends in the mayor's office without knowing any details. I guess that's the physician in him. He always has to be in charge."

"But you have a good relationship with your father," PJ said.

"Anyone can have a good relationship with *Doctor Smith* if they do whatever it takes to please him. I'm fortunate that I was blessed with exceptional athletic skills and a high IQ. Poor Timmy was not as fortunate and was always in Dad's doghouse. The only way Timmy could get attention from him was by rebelling. Just like tonight. He didn't stay at the game, not because he was jealous of me or angry with me, but to make our father upset."

PJ twisted her legs in the seat so she could face Joshua. "Don't you dare blame yourself for Timmy's problems! He didn't feel that way. He worshipped you."

Tears welled up in Joshua's eyes. It was impossible not to think of the bad hand life dealt to Timmy.

Joshua turned off the blacktop highway onto the narrow graveled road that led down to the lake. He recalled the picnic spot and happier times when he and PJ brought Timmy with them on picnics and to swim in the lake during the summer. Timmy had been nine years old when Joshua and PJ started dating in their freshman year at Clark Central High School.

For the past year, Timmy had treated PJ as his sister even though she and Joshua had not set a wedding date. Joshua hadn't given PJ an engagement ring until the beginning of his senior year at UGA—after much prodding by his mother and Timmy. His father was cool to the idea, suggesting that Joshua wait until he finished medical school before considering marriage. That suggestion was not well accepted by anyone else in the family.

Joshua was familiar with the area where the three frightened teenagers awaited him. He negotiated several turns on the narrow road before he saw Timmy's Jeep, an exact replica of his own. Black, with red interior, and equipped with both a hard and soft top. His heart was in his throat as he approached the area. He parked behind his brother's twin Jeep, switched off the engine and sat quietly, attempting to compose himself. After a few minutes, he opened his door, motioning for PJ to stay inside.

"Wait here until I talk to Eddie."

Eddie Hubbard climbed out of the Jeep when Joshua approached. The girls remained in the back seat.

Joshua walked closer and saw Eddie's swollen red eyes. His voice cracked. "Where is Timmy?"

Eddie led him through a thick cluster of tall pines to a grassy spot about twenty feet from the edge of the water. A dented Coleman cooler and several empty beer bottles marked the spot where a few hours earlier, the four teens were enjoying life. A few feet away lay Timmy's covered body.

Joshua pulled back the edge of the blanket. Dropping to his knees, he placed his hands on his brother's face and recoiled from the cold, clammy feeling of the skin. A cry of anguish burst from his lips. He leaned forward, picked up the thin body and cradled him in his arms. He rocked back and forth, his heart pounding in his chest, tears streaming down his face as he wrestled with the harsh reality.

"Oh my God, little brother. How am I going to tell Mom?"

It was several minutes before he heard the sobs of the others and looked up into the grief-stricken faces around him. He couldn't imagine the horror Eddie and the two girls had experienced during their futile efforts to save their friend.

Joshua laid Timmy's head back onto the jacket. Brushing some pine needles from his brother's hair, he bent forward and kissed the cold forehead.

Maria sobbed and fell prostrate onto the lifeless body.

Joshua caressed Maria's hair, as he quietly wept. He didn't know Maria or Lisa and his memory of Eddie was vague, but at that moment, he felt a special closeness to all three. They were Timmy's friends.

Finally, he motioned Eddie to step away from the girls. PJ had come up and was hugging them.

"Tell me exactly what took place, Eddie. Don't leave anything out to protect Timmy or the three of you. It will be best if I get the facts straight before I call the police. They will ask a lot of questions and for all your sakes, your answers must be the same."

Eddie, sounding composed now, told Joshua everything that happened from the time they had arrived at the lake through the episode of Timmy's final seizure. He hesitated when he told Joshua about the brown powder. "I didn't see him use it, but Maria said he took the powder out of a small plastic bag and sniffed a bunch up his nose."

Eddie swallowed hard. He placed his hand on Joshua's arm and broke down. "I wish it was me. He was a friend like I had never known. I would take his place if I could."

Joshua saw genuine pain in Eddie's eyes and knew it was the truth. "I don't blame any of you for what happened. I knew some people at the university used drugs but I had no idea that Timmy did. My parents will have a hard time believing it. My father, especially, will blame you. I don't," he said.

"The people who took Timmy's life are the scum selling the drugs. They make sure it is available for kids like Timmy, who are too immature to use common sense. I know they didn't force him to use it, but their greed was the cause of his death. They will be dealt with, in time."

Joshua turned toward his Jeep to get his cell phone. Walking away, his shoulders slumped, he spoke quietly to himself.

Eddie heard his remarks and felt the hair on the back of his neck bristle. He reached out to the others who had moved to his side.

"What did he say?" Lisa asked.

Eddie seemed puzzled. "I'm not sure. I didn't hear all of it. Something like 'as you sow…'"

Joshua and PJ leaned against the back of his Jeep as they awaited the arrival of the police. Joshua had instructed Eddie and the girls to remain in Timmy's Jeep until he signaled for them. Exhausted and in shock, they complied.

Joshua held PJ against his body, his muscular arms encircling her waist. He pulled her face into his thick flannel shirt, stroking her long chestnut-colored hair. Since their first date, he had doted on the beauty of her hair, so she never cut it and now it reached to her waist.

He noticed that she was shivering and instinctively knew it wasn't from the coolness of the night. He was aware that she was hurting also. She and Timmy had bonded quickly, almost from the day she first visited the Smith family.

Surrounding the lake were several hills covered with tall pine trees lining the slopes and down the shallow banks to the water line. The trees and the winding road obscured the approach of the police vehicle until the beams from the headlights of the Ford Explorer SUV flashed across the grass leading to the water's edge.

Joshua waved his arms to attract their attention, and stepped away from PJ into the bright light from the vehicle.

When the white SUV stopped several feet behind his Jeep, Joshua noticed the insignia of Greene County Deputy Sheriff on the driver's door. He had been correct thinking that the area next to the lake was in Greene County's jurisdiction.

A giant of a man stepped out of the passenger side of the vehicle, placed a wide-brimmed hat on his head and walked toward Joshua.

The driver remained in the vehicle with the car's radio handset up to his mouth.

The big man gave a hand signal to the driver, adjusted his hat and nodded to Joshua. "Are you the fellow that called 911?"

Joshua stuck out his hand, which the deputy grasped. "Yes, sir. My name is Joshua Smith." As he spoke, he handed his driver's license and UGA student ID card to the deputy.

The deputy looked over the cards and returned them. "I know of you, young fellow. You play quarterback for the 'Dogs. Good game against Tennessee tonight. We caught most of it on the radio between calls."

Joshua nodded in acknowledgement and returned his cards to his wallet.

"I'm Rufus Johnson, deputy sheriff of Greene County. The 911 dispatcher referred the call to us since we patrol this area of the lake. What happened and how did you get here from the game so fast? And why?"

Joshua took a deep breath to steady his voice. "My brother was hanging out here with some friends, and from their description, he had a seizure and died."

"You said 'from their description,' so I take it, you weren't here when your brother died?"

"No, sir. I was still in the locker room at Sanford Stadium, showering after the game. I checked my cell phone and found a text message from Eddie, one of my brother's friends. He was here with Timmy, along with their girlfriends. They were having a picnic while they listened to the ballgame. I told the three of them to wait in my brother's Jeep until you arrived. They had attempted to resuscitate my brother and when they couldn't, they panicked, called me and left the message. They told me they had called 911, but I learned that wasn't the truth. They were scared to death and weren't thinking rationally."

The deputy walked over to the other Jeep and looked inside as he played the beam from his flashlight across the frightened faces. He returned to Joshua and motioned for him to continue.

"I came out here after I read the message. I'm familiar with the place. I've been here many times with my girlfriend." He gestured toward PJ.

For the first time, Deputy Johnson made eye contact with PJ, nodding his head as he touched the brim of his hat. He excused himself, walked back to the SUV and leaned into the open window. He spoke to the driver and the headlights were switched to low beams. The deputy returned, removed his hat, and rubbed the crown of his shaved head as he continued his questioning.

"Has anyone else been out here?"

Joshua swallowed the bile in the back of his throat. "No, sir. When I arrived, Timmy's friend … uh … Timmy is my brother's name. Anyway, Timmy's friend, Eddie, and their girlfriends were huddled together next to the body. I asked them to back away while I checked Timmy. He was already cold and stiff. I held his head against my chest—otherwise I didn't move anything."

Johnson rubbed his head again as he stared first at the Jeep containing Eddie and the girls, and then at Joshua. The deputy had had years of experience in dealing with tragedy and in asking questions. "You and your lady friend remain here while I take a look at your brother." He started to say something else, stopped, and walked toward the lake.

Joshua watched as the deputy strolled around Timmy's body

without touching him. Several times the man bent over to examine something but left everything in place. When the driver tapped on the horn, Johnson returned to the vehicle and conversed for several minutes with the driver who remained inside. He gestured to the driver before he returned to Joshua and PJ.

Clearing his throat, he paused, as though carefully selecting his words. "I found alcohol containers and drug paraphernalia around the body. These kids look under age. We have to handle this area as a crime scene, and my partner has called the investigators from the Drug Task Force and the crime scene personnel. We'll stay here until they arrive to maintain the integrity of the site."

Joshua stared at the deputy, a look of disbelief on his face. "Do you suspect my brother's friends did something to him? I can't believe that."

"Okay, easy now. I know you are shook up but this is standard procedure. No one is accusing anyone of anything. We have protocols we have to follow and as painful as it can be sometimes, we still have to follow them."

Joshua dropped his head in acceptance. He felt PJ place her arms around his waist and he pulled her closer. His mind was shutting down and he almost missed the deputy's next question.

"Did your brother have a history of seizures?"

Joshua's pulse quickened. The time for the awful truth had arrived. "No. To my knowledge, this was the first time ever. I need to tell you something else. I think Timmy used cocaine, along with a lot of alcohol."

The deputy gestured toward the other Jeep. "What about the other kids, they doing stuff, too?"

"They had alcohol and Eddie told me the girls were doing Ecstasy, but I don't think they got into the cocaine."

The deputy's face softened. "We'll need to question them at some point but I don't have the manpower to do it at the moment. I'm sorry about your brother. It could have been a case of OD but sometimes they just get unlucky and get a batch of bad stuff. The scum that sells this stuff cut it with all kind of crap to increase the volume and up their profits. Not the kind of people who care what happens to the user."

Johnson waved Joshua toward the other vehicle. "I appreciate your cooperation and I would like for you and your lady friend to join the others. Tell them to remain in the Jeep. After I make a few calls I'll be over to talk to them. Geographically, we are in Greene County's jurisdiction but we don't have the manpower to handle drug cases that involve death, so the investigators from Clarke County will be the ones to handle things."

Joshua choked up as he thought of his parents. "My father is a physician in Athens and he might be at Athens Regional or St. Mary's Hospital. He makes his hospital rounds late after the games or he might be in one of the emergency rooms. Please don't use Timmy's name on the radio. I don't want my father to learn about his son's death from some clerk in the emergency room."

The deputy put his hand on Joshua's shoulder, his touch gentle. "I won't mention names on the radio and I'll see to it that the others don't as well. Since you live in Athens, I'll ask the Clarke County people to accompany you home to see your folks. It'll be a while though. I know it will be painful but the detectives will have a lot of questions for your friends before we leave the scene. After they finish here, they'll take them to the Clarke County jail until they locate their parents."

PJ gasped at the thought of the young girls being locked up. "Is it necessary that they go to jail?"

The deputy explained. "Sorry. I didn't mean to imply they would be incarcerated. They will be held in one of the offices of the Juvenile Division until their parents are located and arrive to pick them up. Didn't you say they were all from Clarke County?"

Joshua's voice was strained. "Yes. They all go to the same high school. God! They are just kids."

The deputy nodded. "That will make it a lot easier. I'll turn them over to the investigators. They will see that their parents are notified. Doug Anderson and Marvin Billings are the chief investigators on the Drug Task Force. They're good men and won't give your friends a lot of hassle. This late, I don't think we'll have to worry about any reporters out here, either."

The mention of the news media shook Joshua. For the first time, he thought of the team and the remainder of the promising football season. How would he stay focused? How would it be possible for him to play a game under these circumstances?

CHAPTER 6

A beige Ford four-door sedan, hidden by a dumpster, was parked in an alley adjacent to a convenience store. The night air was cool, but inside the car it was hot and muggy. The pungent odor of the garbage and dried urine behind the large container made it imperative to keep the windows up, adding to the discomfort of the occupants.

Doug Anderson and Marvin Billings spent many nights on stakeout, futile attempts to nab a supplier to the street dealers in hopes of busting up the whole supply chain. The jail cells were full of the less important street punks, illegal Hispanics and worthless blacks who plied their illicit trade on the streets.

Billings could stomach the illegal Hispanics, but his black brothers made him want to puke. At some point in their childhood, someone should have kicked their sorry asses and got them back on the right track. Unfortunately, too many used their race as an excuse to seek the easy way to money and blamed their misdirection on society.

The two men had been partners for nearly fifteen years, only five years less than Billings' total time on the force. Although he had seniority on Anderson, he was below him in rank because of Anderson's education—a master's degree in criminal justice. Billings had received most of his training as a military policeman during his stint with the U.S. Army. He joined the Athens police after his discharge and from there gravitated to Clarke County. After serving as a jailer, he spent a couple of years as a patrolman. His dedicated service got him promoted to deputy, and then to his present position as a detective on the Drug Task Force.

Anderson slammed his fist against the climate control panel of the county-issued car. He grinned when the fan motor started up again with a death rattle. "This piece of shit is worse than my own car. You would think someone in the department would have pity on us and give us a car that would make this job a little more bearable."

Billings responded with a toothy smile, amused at his partner's antics. He ran his hand over his salt-and-pepper short hair before reaching over with his massive hand to squeeze the back of Anderson's neck playfully. "Take it easy, Doug. If that air conditioner dies from your percussion maintenance, we'll be forced to roll down the windows and enjoy a larger dose of the bouquet of this godforsaken place."

The two of them had been parked for just over three hours amongst the dilapidated warehouses alongside a branch of the Oconee River. Few of the city's elite ever saw this section of the city, so it made an ideal location for drug runners to transfer their products to the local pushers. An anonymous caller had tipped them that a big load was being brought in to one of the warehouses for distribution.

"Looks like another wild goose chase," Billings said. "At least we got to hear most of the Bulldogs' victory over Tennessee. You can thank the maintenance people for repairing the radio." He laughed at his own attempt at humor. "You know, that Smith kid is doing a great job at quarterback. I've heard talk that he might be a first-rounder in the NFL draft this spring."

Anderson glanced over at his partner, whose six-foot-six-inch, three-hundred-fifty-pound frame filled the passenger side of the car. Their fellow officers at the department compared them to Mel Gibson and Danny Glover of "Lethal Weapon" fame because of their personal contrast in appearance and demeanor. Anderson carried his two hundred and twenty pounds on a five-foot-ten frame. He wasn't small by comparison to the average man, but next to Billings, he was both height and weight challenged. He wore his blond hair in a Fifties-style crew cut that gave his peers even more ammunition to zing him. He was feisty and quick to anger whereas Billings kept a cooler head.

"Damn all, Marvin. When are we going to catch a break on these guys? We've been on these bullshit stakeouts for months, with nothing to show for it."

Billings retrieved a handkerchief from his back pocket, no easy feat in the close confinement of the car. He wiped the sweat from his brow. He could feel the moisture soaking his shirt and pants at the small of his back and the discomfort from sitting in one place for three hours helped him understand his younger partner's impatience.

"It'll come. These guys have been pretty smart so far. They must have good leadership, but sooner or later, the luck will swing our way and we'll get the break we need to nail their collective asses to the barn door. We just have to be patient and wait for that break."

Anderson's reply was interrupted by a sudden bark from the car radio.

"Unit Twelve. Dispatch here."

Anderson picked up the hand piece, glad for any change in the boring routine. "This is Unit Twelve."

"Unit Twelve. We have a call from the Greene County Sheriff Department. They have a suspicious death, possible drug related, at a location on Lake Oconee. They have a vehicle with two officers on location. I'll patch you through to them for directions."

"Got you, Dispatch. We're leaving our position on stakeout and we'll check back in after we get on location."

Anderson shrugged, looking toward his partner. "That location is out of our district, but what the hell. It beats sitting here doing nothing but smelling garbage."

Neither of the men appreciated the irony of the moment. The break they wanted so much had just been dumped into their laps.

CHAPTER 7

A fine mist, like freshly shed tears, fell from the mottled gray sky and was ignored by the crowd of teens and athletes who remained at the grave site to whisper their condolences to Joshua. The adults had paid their respects and left quickly, seeking respite from the inclement weather. Joshua's mother, Constance, weakened by her grief to the point she could no longer stand without assistance, had been taken home by Dr. Smith, her husband. The younger generation was less concerned by the weather and delayed their departure for a chance to speak to their friend and sports hero.

PJ stood with Joshua, her arms around his waist, and her face buried in the lapel of this coat. A teammate spoke and she looked at the expression on Joshua's face, amazed at his stoicism. The tragic event coupled with the pressure from the football schedule and his mid-term exams would be enough to drive most men to their knees. She knew Joshua was strong but she worried his outer appearance of acceptance masked inner chaos.

She was close to the entire family, with the exception of Dr. Smith, who always appeared out of sorts due to her presence. She loved Constance Smith almost as much as her own mother, and she had been like a sister to Timmy.

As PJ held Joshua, she feared most what she could not see. This was not the same person who cried without shame when he told her of the manner of Timmy's death. Now he was overwhelmed with guilt. He had ignored the warning signs of his brother's drug use and blamed himself for not recognizing Timmy's aberrant behavior even though they had been together only a few days each month.

She suffered even worse guilt. A few days before his death, Timmy had told her about his drug use. He felt safe discussing things with her and they had a long discussion about medical and legal risks. He had made her promise not to tell Joshua and she hadn't betrayed his trust. Fearing Joshua's reaction, she was afraid to tell him now. Would he reject her?

Joshua stiffened and she raised her gaze to his face, just as Eddie approached them. She dropped her arms to her sides and grasped

Joshua's hand.

Attempting to speak, Eddie stuttered. "Josh…sh…ua. You may not want to talk to me but I wanted to tell you again how sorry I am about Timmy. He was my best friend."

Joshua's shoulders slumped. "I told you at the lake, I don't blame you for what happened to Timmy. I blame myself more than anyone else. He was my kid brother. It was my responsibility to watch over him."

Eddie's eyes were wet and his voice quivered. "He worshipped you, Joshua. He wasn't a jock like you but he was proud of everything you did. He didn't do drugs because he was depressed or unhappy with his life. He just liked to cut up and act crazy. We never did anything bad. I don't know why he got that new stuff."

Joshua placed his hand on Eddie's shoulder. "I know you feel the pain I feel. We'll get together later and talk. I have some questions you might be able to answer. I'm sorry we never got to know each other better when Timmy was alive. Stay in touch with me."

After the last of the mourners left, Joshua and PJ walked hand in hand to the edge of the grave. As they stood beside the flower draped casket, Joshua noticed for the first time the workers who were standing yards away waiting for everyone to leave so they could lower the casket into the vault. They stood silently in the rain. Joshua nodded his appreciation for their patience, reached down and grabbed a handful of soil from under the artificial green carpet placed around the vault. Together, he and PJ tossed the wet dirt on the casket.

Joshua placed his arm around her. She shivered. For the past few days she had been tough, he thought. She was wet and cold but never complained and never left his side.

When they reached the limousine, the driver got out and opened the back door. Joshua helped PJ into the limo before he glanced one last time at the casket that held his beloved little brother. Looking away from the painful scene he noticed two men in tan raincoats further up the hillside under the limbs of a massive oak. The taller of the men was black and appeared in conversation with his white companion.

Joshua stared at them for several moments before he recalled the two investigators who had questioned him that night at the lake. He climbed into the limo, sitting close to PJ, curious why the detectives were standing in the rain to watch the funeral.

CHAPTER 8

Constance Smith wiped at the tears streaming over her high cheekbones. Her usually beautiful, exotic eyes were swollen, and dark circles showed underneath from the continuous bouts of crying since the death of her younger son. She sat on his bed surrounded by his personal things, staring at the posters of his favorite rock group, Kiss, that hung on one of the walls. The other three walls were covered with posters and blown-up photographs of Joshua taken by sports photographers over the years.

At Timmy's desk were stacks of picture albums containing photos of him from infancy to a recent family outing. Everything she touched and saw made the memory of him more vivid, yet she could not bring herself to put his things away.

She had been partial to Timmy since the day his frail body came from her womb. The images of the delivery were still frozen in her mind since she had been awake throughout the procedure, refusing any pain medication because the fetal monitor revealed evidence of distress. After the delivery, the obstetrician and pediatrician had worked frantically over the cyanotic baby, lying so lifeless on the table next to her. Minutes had seemed like hours until a shrill cry came from the tiny body; after she said a silent prayer, she allowed the nurses to give her medication to relieve her discomfort.

Reflecting back, she was never able to determine why Timmy had been such a sickly child while his brother had been so robust. It had been apparent from early childhood that Timmy would not have the athletic build or skills of his older brother, so she made a larger place in her heart for him, to make up for her husband's obvious worship of Joshua. She loved Joshua just as much, but he never needed her attention like Timmy.

Even now, James did not seem to grieve for their lost son as she did. He was a good provider but had never been very loving toward her or Timmy. He was cruel to Timmy, not in a physical manner, but his criticism wounded his son and left deep emotional scars.

Constance walked to the window and stared at the massive live oak trees that lined the street, thinking of the fairytale life she had experienced to this point. She lived in a beautiful home in an upscale neighborhood. She was married to a doctor and had two beautiful children. All that changed the night the police arrived with Joshua and PJ and with the horrible news. Later, when she learned the manner of Timmy's death, she blamed herself and thought of herself as an unfit mother.

Why had he turned to drugs? He had always confided in her, from his first heartbreak in the third grade to his anxiety over entering high school. Was she such a terrible mother that she couldn't sense the pain her offspring was experiencing? Her heart ached, not just from the grief of his death, but also from the knowledge that her son was suffering and she hadn't seen it or heard his cries for help.

Constance left the window and returned to Timmy's bed. She collapsed on the soft comforter and sobbed until, exhausted, she fell asleep.

CHAPTER 9

James Smith stood at a pay phone in a strip mall in east Athens. It was late evening; most of the small shops were closed. The exception was a mini-market that remained open for customers needing gasoline, cigarettes, beer and sundry items. An apparent shift worker was at the checkout counter with his purchases. No one appeared to notice the unimposing short Caucasian man dressed in khaki pants and a long-sleeved flannel shirt. It would be improbable that anyone would recall his presence that night.

Smith dropped a few coins in the phone, listened for the dial tone and punched in ten digits. Exactly six rings later someone answered. He didn't wait for identification; there was only one person who would answer the number he dialed. "Manuel, do you recognize my voice?"

A deep voice resonated over the line. "Yes, boss. I'm clear on this end."

"Talk to me, Manuel. I want to know what happened. There are no reports of other teen drug-related deaths. How did our supply get contaminated?"

The man on the other end of the line replied in a quivering, barely audible voice, the bravado gone.

Smith leaned hard against the aluminum phone booth, pressing the receiver firmly against his ear. "Speak up, Manuel. I want some answers! Poisoned kids will kill our distribution. If this is an isolated case, I want to know how the poison got mixed in that particular buy and who was responsible. I'll be back in touch in forty-eight hours. Have something for me, or we might have to take a trip to Atlanta together."

Manuel coughed and gagged, digesting the information.

Good, thought Smith. The more Manuel feared facing Ortega, the quicker he would find out who was trying to sabotage their operation.

"I'll have it for you, boss. I might have to rough up a few people but I'll find out what's going down."

Smith relaxed, the tension gone from his voice. "We've had a good four years together and we've made a lot of money, but there's more to be made, so let's make sure nothing interferes with our operation."

He hung up the phone, checked his watch, and walked two blocks to his Mercedes parked in front of a BellSouth retail store. He thought about his conversation with Manuel. Their area of distribution was large, even for a college town, but it had grown even larger over the past year with the success in penetrating the high schools. He had to give that credit to Manuel who brought in people able to pull it off.

The increase was good for business but bad for control. It required too many small dealers, a majority of them Hispanics who were in the country illegally. It was almost impossible to check up on them or know of their personal habits and lives since they didn't remain in one place. Smith had to rely on scum like Manuel to do it. That was a problem. Manuel had proven on more than one occasion that he wasn't trustworthy. It was necessary to keep him on a tight leash. His position was mandatory as Smith couldn't expose himself. Things would get sorted out, one way or another.

Using the illegal immigrants as small dealers had a good side. They were virtually invisible to the government and left no paper trail. They followed orders; they knew doing otherwise would get them, at best, a trip back to Mexico. However, they were all poor and anxious to live the American Dream, so each of them tried to find ways to make an extra buck.

Often, someone down the distribution line stretched out their small supply by cutting the cocaine with other products that appeared similar. Powdered milk, sugar and strychnine were favorites. Done right, they didn't cause much harm—a bad hangover, maybe—but if the mix was done haphazardly, a disaster like they were dealing with now could occur. If no other cases showed up, Manuel could trace the source of the problem to the last dealer who moved the drug.

Smith thought of the revenge he would extract from some wetback that endangered his organization.

He smiled.

The death of his son never entered his thoughts.

CHAPTER 10

Eddie climbed to the top of the metal stands at the west end of the UGA Bulldogs' practice field. The sun was low in the sky behind him, the long shadows a signal that practice would soon be over since the large banks of lights around the field were still dark.

He looked over the players, unsure which was Joshua, but he saw four players standing in a group away from the remainder of the team. All four wore red singlets over black jerseys and they stood out from the sea of white practice jerseys, like a redhead in a room full of blonds. These guys were the quarterbacks, the nucleus of the team. The red singlet was a sign, "Do not damage."

Eddie noticed one player among the four was taller, more muscular. That was probably Joshua. Eddie recalled that after Joshua took Clarke Central High School to the State Championship during his senior year in high school, he was aggressively recruited by UGA, and when he signed with the Bulldogs, being a home town boy, he was a popular choice both with the fans and with the coaches.

Eddie was uneasy, meeting with Joshua. He was aware that Joshua knew little of him, other than what they had discussed at the lake and at the graveside, but he knew plenty about Timmy's big brother. Eddie could not recall a time when he and Timmy were together that the subject of Joshua didn't come up. With all Joshua's sports and academic accomplishments to brag about, those were not the things Timmy had mentioned. Instead it was about the times Joshua had taken him to concerts to see his favorite performers, or trips to Six Flags, White Water and other fun places. Eddie had often envied Timmy, with his well-to-do parents, his sports-hero brother, but that was now in the past.

He had no idea what Joshua wanted but when PJ gave him the message to meet Joshua after practice, he hadn't hesitated. The coroner's inquest had ruled the cause of Timmy's death was from cerebral anoxia, a result of the seizures brought on by the use of the tainted cocaine. The medical examiner had found significant amounts of strychnine in Timmy's urine, blood and gastric contents.

The investigation was over quickly even though the authorities knew there was no way the strychnine was in the cocaine by accident. The detectives asked a few questions before they accepted the stories of Eddie, Maria and Lisa. Rumors floated around the school for a time but it quickly became old news and the students soon lost interest.

Eddie surmised correctly that Dr. Smith used his influence with the Police Commissioner and the local politicians to keep the affair low key, since underage girls were involved. It wasn't hushed up as any favor to Eddie or the girls.

His thoughts were interrupted by a commotion on the field. The players began chanting and clapping their hands as they gathered around the coaching staff. Whatever was revealed was well received by the players, who screamed even louder and broke into a hard run for the field house.

Eddie leaned against the wooden seat behind him to wait. Watching the players sprint from the field, he noticed one of the players wearing a red singlet turn toward him and wave.

Eddie did likewise.

The sun was below the level of the bleachers before the first of the players came out of the athletic field house. Eddie left his seat and drifted toward the players' parking lot. Joshua was among the last of the players to leave. He walked with his backup quarterback into the parking lot. They stopped just short of his Jeep, spoke a few words and separated. Although he had requested the meeting, Joshua was not sure what to ask or at least how to say what he had in mind without scaring Eddie to death.

Eddie stepped away from the Jeep when Joshua approached. He appeared calm, standing with his hands stuffed in the back pockets of his jeans. He probably remembered James Dean standing that way in an old TV movie, Joshua thought.

Joshua pitched his back pack into the Jeep. "I'm glad PJ got in touch with you—thanks for coming."

"No problem," Eddie said.

Joshua made eye contact with him. "The name Carlos Sanchez mean anything to you?"

"It depends." Eddie looked away, folding his arms across his chest. "What do you need to know about him?"

Joshua noticed the defensive stance and softened his tone. "I'm sorry. I think I started this off all wrong. I didn't intend to sound like a prosecutor. I have reason to believe Timmy was getting drugs from a guy named Carlos. I just assumed you might be able to shine some light on that subject for me."

Eddie dropped his arms. "I'm sorry as well. I mean, I'm sorry I acted like a bad ass. Timmy was my best friend—in fact, my only true friend. He did things for me no one else ever did, including my own family." His voice broke. "He ... he treated me like an equal even though I'm from a different side of the tracks. I miss him a lot. I'll help you any way I can."

Joshua recognized the emotion in the voice. From that moment, he knew he would no longer be alone in his quest.

Eddie regained control, his voice stronger. "Timmy and I both knew Carlos. He's a small time street dealer who sold us grass and Ecstasy. We never bought much from him because his supply was limited but he was the only dealer we knew."

Joshua swallowed hard, dreading the answer to his next question. "Was Timmy a heavy user?"

"No. We did alcohol most of the time but we found that grass and Ecstasy got the girls in a playful mood much quicker. We never used a lot. That stuff Timmy used the night he died was the first time ever. I didn't even know he had it until he mentioned it at the lake. I told him to leave it alone and he left it in the Jeep, but Maria said he went back and got it when Lisa and I were in the water."

"A lot of your friends turned on to this stuff?"

"More than you would imagine. I've been clean since Timmy died but a bunch are still using. Carlos is still around. I see him almost every day at the usual hangouts."

Joshua felt sick. He leaned against the door for support. "I let Timmy down. Maybe he needed my help and I just didn't listen."

Eddie shook his head, grabbing Joshua's arm. "Don't beat yourself up. Timmy thought you were the greatest person in the world. Sure, he had problems with his father but it wasn't like he was using drugs to escape reality. He just liked to have a good time. He would still be here if Carlos hadn't given him that damn stuff, whatever it was."

Joshua fought back his anger. "I heard one of the detectives tell my father that it was Mexican cocaine, cut with powdered sugar and strychnine. Both of the substances that were added are white powders and the sugar covered up the bitter taste of the strychnine. That's what caused the seizures."

Eddie turned toward the hood of the Jeep, laid his head on his arms and sobbed. His voice cracked when he was able to speak. "I heard about it already. I looked up strychnine at the library and everything I read fit the things that happened to Timmy, but I don't believe Carlos would do that to Timmy. I mean, we all got along good and he was always so friendly to us. Every night when I close my eyes, I see Timmy writhing on the ground in pain and I feel so helpless, unable to do one damn thing to help him."

"I know how you feel. For days I felt empty, unable to shake the feeling I had missed an opportunity to help Timmy. Now I realize there was nothing I could have done at the time, but there is something I can do now."

Eddie raised his head. "I'm with you, Joshua. I'm with you all the way."

Unable to sleep, Joshua lay in his bed at the athletic dorm. His mind dwelled on the discussion earlier in the evening and something Eddie said still nagged at him. What was it about the new drug?

Wide awake with no possibility of falling asleep, he dressed and left the dorm. Climbing into the Jeep, he shivered from the bite of the cool air. He drove toward his home, deciding to search Timmy's room for clues to any drug source other than Carlos. He had three hours before his first scheduled class. He would have breakfast with his parents to cover the unexpected trip home.

Joshua parked in his usual place but chose to enter the house through the back door rather than the garage. He slipped off his shoes and climbed the stairs in his stocking feet to avoid awakening his parents. He passed their bedroom and was surprised to see the door open. He peeked into the room to see if they were awake but their bed was empty and the covers undisturbed.

He looked down the hall and saw the door to Timmy's room was ajar. He knew what he would find. He eased the door open, glanced inside, and saw his mother curled up in Timmy's bed. Light from a small desk lamp revealed the dried tears on her sunken face. Joshua was alarmed at how much her appearance had changed in such a short time. A lump formed in his throat and his chest tightened as though someone was squeezing the life out of him.

They all had suffered but he recognized that his mother was totally shattered. With her husband busy with his medical practice and her older son at the University, Timmy had been her main focus; now, he too, was gone.

Joshua brushed a strand of hair from her forehead but she did not stir. At each visit he had noticed she was more withdrawn, and he feared that someday she might not come out.

He turned to leave but when he reached the door he looked back at the woman who had given so much of herself to him and his brother. His resolve stiffened even more; life for drug dealers was about to get a lot more precarious.

Joshua descended the carpeted steps and entered the family room in the basement. He stepped onto the deep pile red carpet that was bordered with black trim around the edges of the room. Even before he entered the University of Georgia his family had been big Bulldog fans and decorated the "sports room" in their favorite team colors.

His eyes were drawn to the black walnut stained oak shelves that held trophies from his exploits in baseball, football, basketball and track. There was a special place for his first trophy, awarded when his team finished first in peewee football when he was eight years old. He recalled the look of pride in his father's face when he proclaimed, "It's the first of many trophies to come."

Joshua passed by the shelves and walked to the end of the room where a giant screen occupied the back wall. Beneath it was a cabinet containing a VCR along with hundreds of video tapes of his various games of sport. He knew from past experiences that the only tape of Timmy was when the two of them were playing in the snow one winter and his mother had recorded the event.

Joshua wasn't interested in reviewing tapes. He walked to a floor-to-ceiling gun vault located to the left of the screen. His father was a gun enthusiast and had collected guns throughout his adult life. Joshua spun the combination dial and opened both doors. He inhaled the pleasant aroma of gun oil as he swung the doors wide enough so he could see all the weapons. The shotguns and rifles were located separately in racks on the left side of the vault. The hand guns were displayed on the right side, snugly hung from felt covered pegs. Each was held in place by an elastic strap through the trigger guard.

As he stared at them, he was amazed how these instruments of violence could appear so beautiful. He was familiar with many of the guns as his father had taken him to the firing range many times, at least in the days before he entered college.

After several minutes of studying the weapons, he selected a Glock 19-9mm and a Colt .45 automatic. He shoved the guns in his jacket pocket along with several boxes of ammunition and empty magazines. He closed the doors to the vault and spun the dial to lock them securely.

As he climbed the stairs he realized he was on a course that would alter his life forever. Rather than experiencing anxiety or fear, he was more concerned that he felt no emotions at all.

Joshua was at his computer in his bedroom when he heard a light knock on his door. He clicked off his email and switched off the monitor, leaving the computer on.

His father entered the room, without waiting for an acknowledgement of his knock. "Hello, Joshua. I was surprised to see your Jeep in the driveway. I've been at the hospital all night with a patient in ICU. Did you come home for any particular reason?"

"Uh … no, Dad. I couldn't sleep and decided to come home and have breakfast with you and Mom. I saw your car wasn't in the garage and figured you were at the hospital. I've been killing time on the computer hoping you would get here in time for breakfast before I left for class. We'll have to fix it ourselves. Mom doesn't look capable of cooking this morning."

His father sat down on the edge of the bed. His shoulders drooped and his face sagged, looking fatigued. If he heard Joshua's remarks he showed little evidence of it. "Joshua. What do you know of the drug use at Clarke Central? I realize you've been gone for three years but you are still familiar with some students there, as well as some of Timothy's friends."

Joshua's jaws tightened. It irked him that his father insisted on calling his brother Timothy, when everyone else, including his mother, called him Timmy. It had appeared that his father did it to irritate Timmy and even now, after his death, he continued to mock him.

Dr. Smith continued, not waiting for Joshua's answer. "I've talked with several of my colleagues, and like me, they were surprised the use of cocaine was so rampant in the high school. We expect it at the university level, but not with the younger kids."

Joshua looked at him in disbelief. "Timmy died from the use of a tainted drug. There was no evidence that he had ever used it before. How do you know there's rampant use, as you say, in the high school? Eddie was his best friend, and he swore to me, Timmy used marijuana and recreational drugs, like Ecstasy, but this was the first time he did cocaine. Don't brand him and the other kids."

His father spoke through tight lips. "Maybe you've got blinders on when it comes to your brother. As for Eddie, I wouldn't believe anything he said. I've tried to believe Timothy's involvement was an aberration, that he just got sucked in by an older crowd. Hanging out with people like Eddie didn't help the situation. You and your friends were never involved in drugs, so I guess I chose to believe it wasn't a problem in the high schools. Timothy craved attention. I think he got into drugs to make himself stand out."

Joshua closed his eyes, fighting back his anger. "Timmy didn't use drugs for attention. I think he used them because he felt he couldn't measure up to what was expected of him."

Dr. Smith's head snapped up, his chin protruding in protest.

Joshua wondered if there was any emotion behind his father's controlled face. His father got up to leave the room, then stopped, turning back to face him.

"I grieve for Timothy as much as you or your mother; I just don't show it like others. Maybe I shouldn't say this, but it makes me feel better to work and get on with my life. Maybe you should encourage your mother to do the same."

Shocked, Joshua fired back, "Is that why you came in here, to get me to work on Mom? She's handling it the best she can. We all are."

PJ developed a broad smile when she saw Joshua enter the library. She had been surprised when he called her earlier on her cell phone as they seldom went out on days when he had football practice and sessions in the chemistry lab. She often wondered where he got the energy to do all the things he accomplished in a day.

"Hey, sweetheart," she whispered when he approached the book checkout desk. "If I had known you would be free tonight I wouldn't have volunteered to fill in for Jennifer."

"What time do you finish?"

"Sometime around ten. I'm sorry, did I forget we were doing something tonight?"

"No. I just had an unpleasant conversation with Dad earlier and I needed to cuddle with someone sweet and soft. If you're not available, can you recommend someone?"

"Before I'd do that, I'd take you back in the research stacks and have my way with you."

Joshua looked around to see if anyone could overhear their conversation. "Then I'll wait for you. I need to look up some material anyway. After you get off we can go to the Varsity and get a late night snack."

"I'm not hungry. How about we drive down to River Road and find a place to watch the river flow over the rocks in the moonlight."

"There is no moonlight. It's dark as the inside of a well outside tonight."

"Who cares?" PJ grinned impishly.

Joshua winked at her and walked to the row of computers available to look up catalogued books. He typed in his search request and was surprised at the number of hits that came up. He clicked on several and wrote down the locations. After finding the books and browsing through them, he selected two to checkout. He waited until PJ was away from the desk helping someone in the stacks before he took his selection to the adjacent desk. He had the books checked out and in his backpack before PJ returned.

"Find what you needed, Joshua?"

"Yeah, but she doesn't get off until ten o'clock. Do you mind if I take a rain check on that river watch? I'm a little more tired than I realized."

"Sure. I understand. Will you call me after practice tomorrow?"

"You can count on it." Joshua swung his pack over his shoulder and gave PJ a wave.

Once Joshua was out of the building, PJ pulled up his ID on the computer. She had it memorized as she had checked out books for him so many times in the past. Joshua had been unaware she saw him when he got the books earlier. She stared at the titles. *Street Drugs, Past and Present* and *Illicit Drugs/Big Business*.

CHAPTER 11

Manuel, true to his word, had the information when Smith contacted him forty-eight hours later. "You're not going to like this, boss. The fellow who made the sale to your son is not only our biggest mover but also knows our turf better than anyone." Manuel paused, but hearing no response he continued, "He also sold the most drugs to the high schools. Hell, he looks like a kid."

"What did he say about the contamination of the supply?"

"He said he didn't mix up anything. The drug was already in small bags when he moved it. His handler made up the bags and marked each one specifically for the area to be sold."

Smith was irritated. Handling the problem with the dealer in question would be more difficult than he expected. If the handler didn't cut the cocaine, problems existed further up the line. Why weren't more cases reported?

He returned his attention to Manuel. "Did the dealer admit selling the drug to the kid that died?"

Manuel winced when Smith referred to his own son as "the kid that died" but didn't hesitate. "No question about it. He knows his buyers. He told me the kid was a regular customer but bought only Ecstasy and marijuana. Carlos Sanchez, that's the dealer's name, said he was instructed by his handler to move the cocaine to the kid. Carlos didn't like the idea of selling a marked package to the young kid but he did what he was told."

Smith frowned. "What's the name of the man who oversees the dealers in that area, including Carlos?"

Manuel hesitated on hearing the question. Smith rarely dealt with this kind of information; in fact, he seldom wanted the details. "That would be Pete. Pete Dawson. Tall, white guy with blond hair and a wimpy mustache—you may have seen him at pickups in Atlanta. By the way, he's also Carlos' brother-in-law."

Silence lingered on the line. "You still there, boss?"

The answer was slow in coming but very distinct. "Find out all you can about Pete. I need to know if he has plans to start his own business. I don't like competition."

Manuel smiled. Pete didn't have enough brains to operate a front yard lemonade stand, much less run a competitive business, but he decided to let Smith make that determination on his own. No need to draw attention to himself.

CHAPTER 12

Carlos lifted a cup of steaming coffee to his lips. His hands trembled and the hot black liquid sloshed from the cup. The din from the front of the house was the usual early morning bedlam from his sister's efforts to corral her children out of the house and into the van. The morning routine on school days was always the same, except this morning Pete, his brother-in-law, was already up, sitting across the breakfast table. The simple fact he was up before eleven was an event in itself.

Carlos placed the cup on the table and started to leave the room. Chills went up his spine when he heard a snarl from the table.

"Sit down, Carlos. Have some more coffee while we wait for the kids to leave."

"I am fine. I have my cup already. I need to go."

"Goddamn you. I said to sit down."

Pete Dawson got up from the table and opened a drawer next to the refrigerator. He removed a long stainless steel butcher knife, twisting it in his hands, watching the reflections from the overhead light on the shiny blade while he glared at Carlos. With a sudden movement he plunged it into the table between the two of them.

Carlos scrambled to his feet in a panic, knocking the chair across the kitchen floor. He wanted to run but had no place to go. Sooner or later, he would have to face Pete. His life as an illegal alien was not a secure one. He was at Pete's mercy with no options other than ride out whatever storm was brewing at the moment. He watched Pete's eyes and when the wild look was gone, he sat down.

Pete grabbed the handle of the knife but did not remove it from its embedded position. He stared into Carlos' eyes with a look of burning hatred. "What the fuck have you been up to, you little shit? Manuel was all over me last night. He had his ass chewed by the MAN. The MAN is pissed off about the media coverage of the poisoned cocaine. The MAN doesn't like attention. He likes things to be quiet and routine."

Carlos froze. He hadn't done anything. Pete had set up the bags and had told him where to deliver them, with no indication of his purpose.

Pete leaned back in his chair, enjoying his role as master over Carlos. He wouldn't admit to Carlos that he didn't know the identity of the MAN. Manuel had told him that he was better off not knowing.

Pete was aware Carlos had nothing to reveal, but the street hustler was smart enough to sense he was in trouble. Pete's plans hadn't worked out and he anticipated rough times ahead. Timmy Smith's death meant nothing to him. He wouldn't have cared if all four of the teens had died.

What pissed him off was that Maria had escaped unscathed. The hot Mexican bitch had been his target. He was livid that she willingly spread her legs for that Smith brat but spurned him every time he tried to make advances. He had thrown money, gifts, and promises of good times at her, to no avail. He had set up Carlos to pass the tainted coke and had been sure they would all use it. If they all had died, he would have been satisfied, except for losing four customers.

Carlos stared at the knife in the table top, silent.

"Cat got your tongue?" Pete chided. "You were the last contact with the drug heads. Manuel told me no other cases have been reported. Did you decide to make your own isolated hit? What happened? Those guys put you down or something?"

Pete leaned forward in a casual manner, his elbows resting on the table. Quick as a cat, he reached across the table and grabbed Carlos' arm, twisting it so violently it threw Carlos to the floor. Pete kicked the chair backwards, sending it crashing against the back wall. He pounced on top of Carlos, pounding his face with his large fists.

Carlos rolled into a fetal position, covering his face with his arms and pulling his knees up to protect his belly. His back and sides were exposed and Pete dropped on him, driving his knee into Carlos' unprotected ribs.

Carlos curled into a tighter ball, his chin against his chest. He saw Pete's fist swing in an upper cut, but he couldn't react fast enough to dodge the blow, which split his lip and smashed his nose. Unable to defend himself, he rolled onto his stomach to protect his vital organs. The blows continued to hammer down on him until he begged for mercy.

As quickly as it started, the tirade was over. Pete backed off, stood over Carlos for a moment, then retrieved his chair and sat down at the breakfast table. "You pathetic little turd. I won't let them do anything to you because you are my best dealer. That's the only reason I'm not going to beat you to death and dump your sorry ass at Manuel's feet. The MAN will be pissed for a while but he's a business man. He's more interested in money than the death of that fucking kid. Just stick with me and I'll handle it."

Carlos muttered through his swollen lips, "What do you want me to do?"

"You need to disappear for a couple of weeks. I want you away from Manuel's goons and the detectives. They will pull everybody off the streets for questioning so it's best if you're not available. Once the media gets bored with the story and it's no longer front page news, they'll drop the investigation."

Pete reached into his front pocket and extracted a large roll of bills. Peeling off fifteen of the Ben Franklins, he passed them over to Carlos. "Take that pile of junk you call a truck and drive down to Savannah for a few weeks. You shouldn't have any problems blending in down there. Find a cheap motel south of Savannah, one of those mom-and-pop operations. They got cut off when I-95 was built so they need the business. They won't ask questions or require registration if you pay with cash. Enjoy yourself. Sleep, eat, and watch cable movies. Use a pay phone to call me in a week. I'll tell you when it's safe to come home."

Pete felt better. He would tell Manuel that Carlos split and probably went back to Mexico; that would take the heat off.

CHAPTER 13

Joshua walked into the field house, uncomfortable about returning to football. He was finding his classes difficult all day, and concentrating on football plays would not be any easier. Walking toward the locker room, he met several teammates who were gracious and acted glad to see him back so soon. Halfway down the hall, he heard someone call out his name and he turned to see the quarterback coach come out of the office.

"Smith, I need to talk with you for a second." The coach held the door open for Joshua to enter and when both of them were inside, the coach plopped down in his chair. He motioned for Joshua to sit in one of the plastic chairs in front of the desk.

"Smith, I want to tell you again, from me, the other coaches and all your teammates, how sad we are over your loss. I have two brothers and I can't imagine losing either of them. That's the reason I called you in here."

Joshua frowned in puzzlement, uncertain where the conversation was heading.

"The coaches met and we think it might be best for you to take a week off from practice and be with your family. I'm familiar with the academic load you carry, and how time-consuming it is. You can't skip your classes but you can miss practice this week, and the game on Saturday. Western Carolina has a good team but no depth, and by the second half, they will be gassed. Your backup can handle it and it will be good for Franklin to have a complete game under his belt."

Joshua was stunned. He couldn't believe the coaches were giving him a week off. Reluctant to say much, he stood up, thanked the coach and left the office.

He would put this week to good use.

The parking lot at Clarke Central High School was a gathering point for the kids at lunch break. Students involved in the technical career programs rather than college preparatory left school after the morning classes, to attend jobs as part of their training. A few of the students walked directly to their cars while others lingered, talking trash with their friends, and grabbing a quick smoke.

Eddie sat in the passenger seat of a car owned by Calvin Jenkins, who was behind the wheel. Calvin had hung out with Timmy in the past and now spent a lot of time with Eddie.

Tall and lanky, with red hair and freckles, Calvin was a modern-day Huck Finn. His face was often decorated with a broad smile, the kind that made you wonder what he had been doing just before you entered the room. He had moved to Athens with his mother after she separated from his father. He, like Eddie and Timmy, had found it hard to fit in with the "cool" students, so he gravitated to the two mavericks. Their antics always produced fun times.

Calvin was more silent with his grief than Eddie. He seldom spoke of Timmy's death, but he carried the weight of it just the same.

Eddie was different. He wouldn't let it go. He talked about it every time they were together. Today, he was more animated than usual. He had pestered Calvin until he agreed to meet him in the parking lot at lunch.

"Damn, Eddie. What has got you so wired? Are you smoking funny weed?"

Eddie crushed out his cigarette in the ashtray, and turned toward Calvin. "You know I don't do drugs anymore. Not since Timmy died. Don't act fucking stupid."

Calvin held up his hands in mock surrender. "What's the matter with you? I've never seen you so worked up."

Eddie looked around but no one was close enough to hear their conversation. "If I tell you something, you've got to promise me you will not repeat it."

The look on Calvin's face revealed his disbelief at Eddie's juvenile comments. "Look Eddie. If you want to tell me something, tell me, but stop this high suspense bullshit."

Eddie grabbed Calvin behind the neck, squeezing hard enough to cause Calvin to yelp. "It's not bullshit, man. I mean what I say. You can't tell anyone."

"All right, I promise." He stretched the muscles in his neck to ease the discomfort.

Eddie leaned closer. "You remember talking about getting even with the assholes that killed Timmy?"

"Yeah, but we were just talking trash. There's not much we can do."

A grin spread across Eddie's face. "Don't bet on it. I know somebody who's putting together a plan. We need help. You interested?"

Calvin cocked his head, his eyebrows peaked in disbelief. "What do you mean 'we'—are you already involved in something?"

"Well, not exactly. Just some talk at this stage; but this guy I know, plans to do some stuff either with or without our help."

"I don't know how I can help but count me in. I owe that to Timmy. Who is this person?"

"I mean it." Eddie dropped his voice to a whisper. "You can't tell anyone else until we get the word, promise?"

"Okay, I get the picture. Cross my heart and hope to die, if I tell."

Eddie took in a deep breath, exhaling his answer. "Joshua."

Calvin slammed his fist on the dash of the car. "Holy crap, you mean Timmy's brother, the honcho of the Bulldogs? You're fucking with me."

"I swear, man. It's the absolute truth. Joshua has a plan to work through the little Mexican who sold the stuff to Timmy so he can get to the big shots. He told me he's going to start out small and gradually build up the volume of his buys until he can get higher up the chain."

"So, when he gets higher up, what will he do?"

"He's going to set them up for the Drug Task Force."

"Fuck no, man. I mean, you talking about dealing with some bad dudes. We'd be better off dead than crossing those mean fuckers. I can't believe Joshua is getting involved in this. He's a jock. He's got a pro career for sure or maybe medical school. No way he'll take a chance on blowing all of that."

Eddie scowled at him. "You already a candy ass and we haven't done a thing. I guess I was wrong about you. I told Joshua you would want to help."

"I didn't say I wouldn't help. I just don't think I could handle being around those fuckers without shitting myself. This is some serious crap. I've heard my old man talk about the drug wars in Atlanta and how those dudes fuck each other up."

Eddie slumped down in the seat, his initial bravado waning. "Come on, Calvin. We don't have to shoot anybody or anything like that. I told Joshua about your dad. He wants you to get information for us about the tactics of the SWAT team your dad works with in Atlanta. You know, how they get themselves undercover and things like that."

"I can do that. I've heard my dad talk about it enough," Calvin said. "That's why he and Mom are separated; he lives that shit. Mom finally got tired of staying at home alone all the time and wanted out. Of course, nothing has changed except we live in Athens and Dad lives in Atlanta. She doesn't go out with anyone except when Dad has time off and comes to see us. I don't think she will ever love anyone except him."

Students in the parking lot began moving toward the school building.

"So, are you with us?" Eddie asked.

"I'm in. Just tell me what I need to do."

"Joshua has no plans for us yet, but I'll talk to him. He'll want us to get together after he figures out a time between his football practice and his labs. You and I will have to work around his schedule. Now, remember, don't say a damn word to anybody about this."

"Okay. I don't believe it myself so even if I did tell someone, they would think I was nuts."

"We probably are," Eddie answered.

CHAPTER 14

Carlos flipped on the directional signal, indicating his intention to exit off I-95. The eighteen-wheeler on his rear bumper had dogged him since he first entered the interstate from I-16 near Savannah. The big truck ignored the signal and remained in the far right lane, closing the gap even more between it and the small dilapidated pickup. Carlos cursed the unknown driver for harassing him. He was pushing his old truck to the limits. If the other driver wanted to go faster, why didn't he change to the two open lanes?

The exit to Highway 17 South loomed ahead and Carlos plunged his trunk onto the ramp. The driver of the huge tractor-trailer continued on I-95, the air horn splitting the air. Carlos exhaled a sigh of relief. The last thing he needed was a confrontation with a redneck truck driver.

The exit ramp curved away from the interstate, ending at a four-lane black-top road. The activity and traffic to the northeast looked hectic so after a moment of indecision, Carlos swung the truck into a right turn and continued south on the long straight road. His tense shoulder muscles relaxed as he loosened his grip on the steering wheel.

After traveling about sixteen miles, he turned off onto a two-lane road and saw an area that appeared ideal. Several individual cabins built of rough-hewn wood and roofs covered with asphalt shingles were lined up under century-old oak trees. Massive limbs, draped with long tentacles of Spanish moss, hung low to the ground. The cabins appeared unoccupied, and a single vehicle was parked in front of a cabin brandishing a green neon "Office" sign. Suspended over the door was a white piece of cardboard that read "Vacancy."

Carlos entered the office through a screen door hanging crooked on its hinges and spotted with several puffs of cotton imbedded in the screen. He stared at the cotton, puzzled about its purpose.

"The cotton plugs holes so the gnats and mosquitoes can't get through the screen." The words seemed to come from nowhere but the source was soon revealed when a small, balding man, carrying a large black cat, entered from a back room. "Need directions?"

Carlos smiled at the chubby old man. "No. I look for a place to stay a few days."

"My name is Doyle Strickland. This fat varmint is VC," the old man said, indicating the cat in his arms. He gave Carlos a once-over. If he noticed the bruises on Carlos' face he made no mention of them.

"You looking for work? Wasting your time, I have to tell you. Not much happens around here since they put in I-95. This use to be a real busy place but as you can tell, we don't get much business anymore. I should have left a long time ago, but when my wife died, I thought, what the hell, I don't have much time left myself, so I decided to stay put. I don't need much excitement anyway."

Carlos immediately liked the old man, taken by his quick to the point attitude. "I no look for work. Just need a place to relax for a few days."

"Well, you could have fooled me. You don't look like the stressed-out businessman type, but if it's relaxation you want, this is a good place for that. Not much action around here and you'll have to go back up to the interstate to find a place to eat. All the restaurants on this stretch of highway closed several years ago. Those what didn't had them mysterious fires in the middle of the night. You know what I mean?"

Carlos nodded. "That will work okay for me. I can get some things at a convenience store. Do the cabins have a kitchen?"

"They do. No oven, but there's two small surface units, a small refrigerator, microwave, counter tops and shelves. Everything works okay, last time I checked. You can't cook a fancy meal but you can fix enough to get by. I do."

Carlos smiled, satisfied with the description. "Good. I pay for a week but I may stay longer." He pulled out a roll of bills, glancing up at Doyle. "I got no credit card. Cash be okay?"

Doyle stared at the wad of money in Carlos' hand, and stammered out the amount. "Let me see. The rate is thirty dollars a night, but since you're paying in cash, make it two hundred dollars for the week." No mention was made of registration or any particular rules regarding the stay.

Carlos dropped the last of the plastic grocery bags on the counter of the small kitchenette. After unpacking his clothes, he made a trip to a Winn-Dixie store he had seen just before he got off the interstate. He had little cooking experience so he had loaded up on canned vegetables, canned meats and packaged crackers.

As he put away his purchases, he thought about the previous few days. Other than his sister and Pete, no one else knew about his departure from Athens, except Rafael. It had required a lot of persuasion but Rafael agreed to take over Carlos' territory and act in his stead. He also understood to feign ignorance of Carlos' whereabouts.

CHAPTER 15

Doug Anderson had decided to be a cop when he was four years old. The decision was dictated by his genes. His father and paternal grandfather had been cops and he had spent hours at their feet listening to exciting tales of car chases and capturing the bad guys.

During his career, he had been the top guy on both the SWAT Team and the Red Dog Team. It was well known by his peers that he was fearless and obsessed with sending drug dealers to prison. An adrenalin junkie, he volunteered for every dirty assignment, and was at the front of every drug bust. A college graduate with degrees in criminal justice and abnormal behavioral psychology, his initial plan was to join the FBI, but a torn-up knee in a touch football game ended that dream.

Instead, he devoted himself to being the best cop on the force. Those who worked with him recognized his driven nature to succeed and his willingness to put in long hours to see that assigned tasks were completed. For those reasons, he was promoted to detective ahead of his peers. His desire to excel left little time for socializing, so he was a bachelor at the ripe old age of thirty-eight.

Anderson despised drug dealers because they preyed on the weak-minded and the poor. Because of this, he spent much of his off-duty time visiting the projects on the south side of town, rapping with the young kids. They avoided him at first, but after he replaced several nets and left new basketballs near the goal posts, they began to warm to him and ran to meet him whenever they saw his black Ford SUV pull into the housing project.

He approached them without demands, never asking specific questions, and soon he was gathering information from casual banter with the kids. He learned that several of the older children were used as mules, carrying drugs onto the school grounds or making drops near the University of Georgia campus. Eventually, he learned the names of those involved. He had a special pity for the kids, caught up in something brought on by the greed of their parents and others.

Anderson pounded his fist on the files that lay open on his desk, splashing coffee from his Atlanta Falcons cup. Heads popped up from several individual cubicles in the crowded office, turned toward him for a brief moment, before looking away with amused grins, familiar with Anderson's intensity and outbursts of frustration.

A stack of paper towels appeared over his left shoulder, followed by the deep voice of Billings. "Are we having a little temper fit?"

Anderson ignored the jibe of his good natured friend. He knew all too well Billings was familiar with his temper, having rescued him many times from the wrath of the administration. Anderson despised regulations that protected the criminals more than the victims. He busied himself cleaning up the spilled mess, resisting the grin that won out and spread across his face.

"Damn all, Marvin. I can't make heads or tails out of the data we have on the last two cases."

Billings nodded. Two street dealers had been found in different sections of the city, their bodies stuffed in garbage dumpsters. Both men were black and had been shot at close range in the center of the forehead with soft-nose bullets from a small caliber weapon.

"Don't get all worked up. Just another drug deal gone bad," Billings said. "Why worry so much about it? That's two less punks on the streets."

Anderson picked up his overturned cup and headed for the Bunn coffee machine in the corner of the office. He motioned for Billings to join him and filled two cups before he answered. "I don't think so. If a druggie had wasted either of them, he would have stripped them of all drugs and money. Both were found with wads of cash and bottles of Ecstasy, crack and a couple of large packets of marijuana."

Taking a sip from his cup, Billings winced. "When was the last time they changed the damn coffee grounds in this machine? This shit tastes worse every time I drink it."

Anderson ignored his partner's comments. "It wasn't a competition hit, either. The blacks are quick with their knives and carve each other up pretty good but there were no knife wounds on either body."

"I agree with you on that. I know my brothers." He laughed. "There's no talk on the street either. No one is bragging about wasting them. None of the street junkies know a thing, or if they do, they ain't talking."

Anderson returned to his desk, dropping into his chair. Billings did likewise at his position across the large desk. They remained silent for several minutes before Anderson spoke. "Have you talked to Carlos?"

"I haven't seen him lately. He might know something, but he's smart enough to realize he might be a target like the rest."

Anderson picked up the coffee-stained files on his desk and read them to refresh his memory.

The first body had been found wedged behind a dumpster at the convenience store at the corner of Hammond and Lee streets. The cop who found the body had reported that the victim was shoved into the small space head first but the size of the body left the feet exposed and the beam from the police car's mounted spotlight fell onto the shiny black patent leather shoes.

Anderson and Billings had arrived within minutes after the call was received at headquarters. They spoke with the cop on the scene, and made notes about the location of the body. It was impossible to do much examination since most of the torso was hidden from view. After noting the exact location and positioning, they pulled the body from behind the large metal container.

Anderson closed his eyes and recalled the moment. He recalled Billings' words.

"Notice anything unusual, partner?" Billings had commented as he circled the body, viewing it from all angles.

Anderson had knelt at the head of the victim, his gloved hands searching for an exit wound in the coarse hair over the occipital area of the scalp. "You mean other than the hole in the center of his forehead?"

Billings chuckled at the black humor, aware his attempt to one-up his partner failed. "No, I mean other than that."

"Well, for one thing, he has rings on at least four fingers and a gold chain around his neck that could be used as an anchor chain for a Boston whaler. This dude must have at least a thousand dollars worth of jewelry on him. That should rule out robbery as a motive. There's no wallet and no identification, but he's got a couple hundred bucks stuffed in his front pockets and several bottles of pills and a package wrapped in plastic that I bet is cocaine."

Billings rubbed his hand across his head, wiping away the beads of sweat. "Crap, this doesn't make any sense. Somebody got close enough to pop him in the head, so he must have known his assailant. These guys don't let strangers walk up to them here on the streets."

Anderson got up, rubbing the soreness from his legs. "I agree with you. I can't believe someone wasted this guy just because he didn't like him. Not in this place. I hope we're not about to have a turf war."

Billings whistled through his teeth, nodding his head in agreement. "Let's round up a few of the street junkies and find out what the word is on the street. We might learn something. Even if we don't, we might at least grab a few new faces. The crime scene crew just arrived. You ready for them to take over?"

"Why not? I'm not accomplishing anything here. Make sure they let us know if they ID the victim. Maybe we can cross-reference him with some known dealers, just to make sure he wasn't invading some other jerk's turf. If that doesn't pan out, we might have another unknown."

"Not like it would be the first, good buddy."

Anderson felt a tug at his arm. He looked up at his partner, who was talking to him in the office.

"Hey, are you still with us?"

Anderson grinned sheepishly. "Sorry, I was just thinking back on the scene at the first hit."

CHAPTER 16

PJ slowed her Honda Accord as she entered the intersection of Baldwin Street and Sanford Drive. She saw a BMW Roadster drive away from the curb on the opposite side of the street. She took a quick glance in the rear view mirror, and made a perfect U turn, driving into the vacant spot. Locating a place to park on a usual day was daunting enough, but today it was divine intervention since she was late for her class, the second time this week.

Her life was always fast paced, with her studies, her part-time job and time spent with Joshua, but since Timmy's death things had gone from fast to hectic. She was concerned about Joshua. His time with football, she accepted; she was used to playing second fiddle to a game that allowed adult men to remain boys. But now something else seemed to possess him, taking him away from her even when she was in his arms. It was so unlike him and she could discern coldness, not present before.

She grabbed her books from the front seat and cut across the lawn in front of Baldwin Hall. Even the usual tardy students were present, making her arrival more conspicuous when she took the only unoccupied seat left—on the front row.

Dr. Bill Roberts, the affable Sociology professor, peered over his half-moon glasses, watching PJ arrange her skirt when she sat down. His eyes roamed over her tanned legs and he gave a quick nod of welcome. He resumed his usual practice of pacing in front of the blackboard as he lectured, a long piece of white chalk clutched in his right hand. He rarely used the chalk to write on the board; instead, he used it like a missile, which he threw at any unsuspecting jock who fell asleep in his class.

PJ was serious about her studies and in spite of her concern over Joshua, she found herself engrossed in the lecture. She had learned to ignore the antics between the professor and the jocks, who took the course for the guaranteed A. Dr. Roberts loved his Bulldogs.

Mark Ashton was one of those students. The massive man-child was the starting right offensive tackle on the team, and it was his job to protect Joshua from having his head caved in by an oncoming defensive end.

Mark gazed at PJ, envious of Joshua's involvement in her life. Not only was PJ a true Southern beauty, but a brainy one as well. Her ability to take concise, to the point notes made her a favorite of the football players, who often asked Joshua to intercede for them and obtain copies of her notes for them to study for the exams.

Mark was not focusing on her mind at the moment. He was staring at her long brown hair, which she wore bundled together and tossed over one shoulder. He looked lower at her breasts that amply filled the pullover sweater. The matching pleated skirt stopped just above her knees and revealed a lot of her shapely legs.

Mark's daydream was interrupted when a piece of chalk struck his desk, to the obvious delight of his fellow students.

Roberts sounded happy as he announced that the class was over.

PJ approached Mark outside the building, knowing that he would be surprised and delighted. "Hey, Mark. How does it feel to be a victim of Dr. Roberts' accurate throw?"

Mark blushed. He always got tongue-tied in the presence of pretty girls, even more so with PJ. "I wasn't asleep. I just wasn't paying enough attention, I guess."

PJ laughed. "Don't let it bother you. You are now included in some great company, including that dope you protect every Saturday."

"You mean Joshua? Has he been zinged by Dr. Roberts?"

"You better believe it. The story is told that the chalk skipped off his desk and popped him in the forehead. His friends told me that he turned red as a beet."

"Thanks, PJ. Telling me that story helps me feel less like a fool. I'm proud to be on any list with Joshua."

She paused for a moment to gather her thoughts. "Mark, do you know if Joshua is having difficulty with the coaching staff or something? He has been so moody lately. He told me that everything is okay, but something other than his brother's death is on his mind."

Mark looked at her curiously and took a moment to answer. "I'm sorry, PJ. I can't help you. I can tell you I don't think it is football related. Joshua was excused from practice and the game for this week. I've seen him around some classes but not on the field."

PJ was stunned. Joshua had not mentioned being excused by the coaches. He hadn't called all week and she assumed his schedule was more crowded than usual, since he was spending time at home with his mother. She thanked Mark and strolled to her car, more concerned than ever over Joshua's sudden change.

CHAPTER 17

There are several enjoyable places to be on a Saturday night in Athens, but the south side isn't one of them. Vandalism was so rampant, the city was reluctant to spend money to improve the area. The street lighting was dim in the best spots and totally dark in the worst, since the lights were smashed within hours after the maintenance people left. Graffiti was everywhere, and few abandoned buildings possessed any intact window panes. The night belonged to the tough kids who roamed the streets, along with a few adults who were there for business.

An unmarked car was parked in the shadows on a side street, with a good view of the project housing. Anderson sipped bitter coffee from a Styrofoam cup, his taste buds long ago decimated by so much of the rancid brew. His eyes were focused on a fire hydrant near the entrance to the project parking lot. According to a teenage girl they picked up two days before, this was a prime pickup point used by the college kids who did not want to venture into the housing project.

Anderson's attention was diverted for a second by a gasp and deep snore from his partner, asleep in the passenger seat. Sleep was a rare occurrence for the two detectives since they spent so many hours on stakeouts. It had become a source of contention between the two partners and fast friends. Billings didn't hesitate to express his opinion, resulting in arguments about the waste of time on the fruitless adventures. Anderson encouraged Billings to go home to his family, but he refused. In spite of their differences of opinion, his partner would not let him sit out in the south side area alone.

Anderson felt this time, they might get lucky. The young girl told them of seeing a white college-age boy come to the project area often—always alone and in a black Jeep. Anderson learned from police reports that the small-time dealers remained in downtown Athens, but the bigger fish came to south side. If the same white kid was showing up here on a regular basis, he was a serious dealer. There was nothing they could make of that single bit of information but it might lead to something bigger. At least that was the logic Anderson used to convince Billings to spend another night in their car.

The night was dark and the little moonlight available was partially blocked by cloud cover. Rain was predicted for the weekend and the air was beginning to feel heavy. The blackness of the night was split by a shaft of light from an open apartment door near the street. A tall figure stood in the light for a few seconds before the door closed and the darkness returned. Another splash of light appeared from a lighter, followed by the red glow from the end of a cigarette.

The beams from a car's headlights shined on the dark asphalt street as it entered the area from the north part of town. The shaft of light flashed from low to high beam and back to low. There were no approaching vehicles from the opposite direction.

Anderson watched the red glow from the tip of the cigarette move closer to the street. He punched Billings, who awoke with a start.

"What…What is it?

Anderson whispered directions of his line of sight, allowing Billings to focus on the same place.

A black Jeep passed by the project, swung into the parking lot of an abandoned small grocery store and reversed directions heading back north. Traveling back to the housing complex, it stopped alongside the fire hydrant.

With the small amount of light available, they saw a black man lean into the passenger window of the Jeep. After a couple of minutes, he withdrew and walked back to the apartment. The Jeep remained parked for several seconds more before driving away.

Anderson waited until the apartment door opened and closed again before he pulled out of his parking place.

Billings spoke with excitement. "I've seen that Jeep before or at least one just like it."

"Big deal," Anderson said, somewhat discouraged by the lack of action at the pickup. "There are at least twenty Jeeps just like it in Athens."

"Yeah, but how many have a tag that reads 'DOG1QB'?"

The comment got Anderson's attention.

CHAPTER 19

PJ walked arm in arm with Joshua to the gazebo in the Smiths' back yard. They climbed the steps to the white structure, settling on a bench that gave them a moonlit view of the kidney-shaped pool. She shivered in the cool night air, tucking herself close to Joshua for his warmth. Troubled by his silence, she looked up into his face. "Where are you, Joshua?"

He stared at her with a puzzled expression. Several seconds passed before he spoke. "Right here with my beautiful sweetheart."

"I don't mean physically, you big dope," she said, giving him a playful shot to his large biceps. "I mean, where is your mind? You've been so distant lately, so quiet and even when we're together, your thoughts are somewhere else. I know you miss Timmy and you are worried about your mom, but I can sense that something else in bothering you."

Joshua took her face in his big hands, tilting her lips up to meet his. Reflections from the underwater pool lights sparkled in her eyes. He kissed the tip of her nose, her cheeks and then her warm mouth, his tongue seeking hers. He felt her respond to the gentle caress of her breasts, the nipples erect.

For several minutes they hungrily sought each other, their hands stroking each other with eager warmth. Their lips parted and Joshua embraced her, his strong arms wrapped around her delicate body.

The words came hard. "PJ, I know Timmy loved you like the sister you would someday come to be. He was more comfortable with you than me or anyone else in my family, including Mom."

Tears filled her eyes. She had loved Timmy as well. Many times she had played the role of older sister for Timmy, giving him advice, usually about girl problems.

PJ had worried about Timmy's insecurity, made worse by the constant verbal abuse from his father. Timmy had revealed to her that many of his "failures" were purposely done to retaliate against his father's harassment. She thought again of Timmy's suspicions of his father, something she had repressed since the funeral. Sooner or later, she would tell Joshua. She just didn't know how to do it without adding to his pain.

She gazed into Joshua's eyes, searching for the answer. "I always felt close to Timmy. Sometimes I felt sorry for him but I tried to remain upbeat. He didn't want pity. We've talked about this many times before, Joshua. What is really bothering you? Please tell me. Maybe I can help."

He took a deep breath. "When you and Timmy talked, did he ever mention someone named Carlos Sanchez?"

PJ stiffened in his arms. She paused, knowing this was the opening she needed to confess to Joshua that she knew of Timmy's use of drugs. She swallowed hard, afraid to say the words. Her usual strength failed her.

"I've met a lot of Timmy's friends but the only Hispanic he ever mentioned was Maria." She began shivering again and she tugged on Joshua's arm. "Let's go back inside. I'm getting cold."

Walking toward the house, she nestled her head against his arm. Women's intuition told her that trouble was brewing and the love of her life might be getting involved in more than he could handle.

Once inside the house, they snuggled together on the sofa. With her head on Joshua's chest, she said, "I love you, but you still haven't told me anything. Why are you interested in this person … uh … Carlos?" She heard Joshua take a deep breath.

"Something Eddie told me got me interested in him."

Alarms sounded in her brain and she wanted to warn him not to get involved in business that should be handled by the police. Instead she blurted out, "Why didn't you tell me you were excused from practice all last week? I was aware you didn't dress out for the game. Where were you those afternoons and evenings? Do you even remember the last time we made love?"

Joshua got up from the sofa, pacing around the room. "Come on. Don't start nagging at me even before we are married. I had things to do, just like you have things you don't tell me about. It's no big deal. Let it go."

In response, she stood, picked up her purse from the end table and started for the front door. She stopped and turned back toward him. "Maybe it's no big deal to you, but when my fiancée deceives me and is reluctant to answer my questions, it becomes a big deal to me. Joshua, whether you realize it or not, our relationship is not the same. Something has consumed you and it's not football. You don't have time for me anymore."

Watching her walk out the door, Joshua felt tears welling up in his eyes. He was wrong and he knew it, but he wasn't about to stop her. He had the right to keep some things to himself.

Anderson backed his car out of Billings' driveway, taking care not to stray from the asphalt. When he was in the street, he saw Billings applaud his successful maneuver. The Billings family residence was not large, a standard three-bedroom ranch style, but it was immaculate with a manicured lawn to match.

Anderson was a frequent visitor to the home, especially at dinner, and on each occasion he got the same grilling from Latisha, Billings' wife, about his bachelorhood and his age. Why did married women always feel compelled to be a matchmaker? The wives of cops were the worst. They were forever plotting to get all the single guys married. Maybe they were more comfortable if their husband's partner was married and less inclined to engage in life threatening situations.

Tonight was special for all of them, not only celebrating Billings' forty-fifth birthday but also the fifteenth anniversary of their partnership. They had the evening off, so they grilled steaks and drank a few beers while telling unbelievable stories of their heroics to Billings' twelve-year-old son, Mansa.

Latisha struggled to keep a straight face but enjoyed the way Mansa's eyes got bigger as the stories became more absurd.

Anderson considered the Billingses his surrogate family and enjoyed his time with them. They felt the same way; the children even called him Uncle Doug. He envied Billings and his happy family, but knew there was no place in his life at the moment for a spouse or family. Maybe in a few years but for now he was married to his job and loved it.

He stopped at the intersection beyond Billings' house, flipped on the left turn signal, intending to turn toward his apartment. He paused for a moment, changed his mind and turned right toward the northern part of town. A short time later he was cruising through Oak Grove subdivision. He saw Joshua Smith getting out of his Jeep and with no particular plan in mind, he pulled into the Smiths' driveway.

His headlight beams flashed across the front of the Smith house, and Anderson saw Joshua stop on the front porch, staring back in his direction. He apparently recognized Anderson's car and approached, stopping at the driver's window.

Anderson left the engine running and got out to greet him. "Evening, Joshua."

"Detective Anderson, something I can do for you?" Joshua's tone was brusque.

Anderson was uneasy since he had not anticipated the impromptu meeting. "Billings and I saw your Jeep around southside Saturday night. I know you didn't dress out for the game because we listened to the game on radio. I'm sure your coaches didn't excuse you so you could hang around the worst area in town."

Joshua glared at him. "I was just riding around listening to the game on the radio. I didn't realize how tough it would be not to dress out. I missed being with the team. I got lost and stopped to ask someone for directions. Is that a crime?"

"No. That's not a crime, but dealing in illegal drugs is a crime. You've been seen in some strange places for a person of your social status and athletic reputation. I don't think your father would approve of the places you've visited recently. I'm certain the athletic department would be very disturbed over some of your activities."

Joshua leaned against the front fender of the detective's car, his arms folded across his chest. "Just how would you know where I've been? You got a tail on me?"

"Don't need to. We have eyes and ears all over this town. Sometimes we develop an interest in certain people and the word gets out. You'd be surprised how helpful some folks can be. Your Jeep is not that hard to recognize, with the vanity tag."

Joshua straightened, stepping toward Anderson. His arms dropped to his side and he curled his fingers into fists. "What's your problem? Why are you on my ass?"

Anderson leaned toward him, so close he had to look up to make direct eye contact. "I've got a problem with you being in areas where known drug dealers hang out. I've got a problem with a boy who lost a brother to drugs even being around where that shit is available. I've got a problem with any kid whose mother has almost lost her mind in grief over the loss of her son, being involved in something that could do her more harm. I've got a problem with a college athlete who is worshipped by a lot of kids being around any of the scumbags that sell drugs and death."

Anderson took a deep breath and shouted in Joshua's face, so close his spittle sprayed him. "I've got an even bigger problem with a bunch of drug dealers who are turning up dead and I don't have a clue as to why."

Joshua backed up and turned toward his house. He paused, looking back at Anderson. "It sounds like you've got problems but unless you have something specific to talk to me about, leave me the hell alone. My father knows people in high places downtown who would be very unhappy if you caused problems with the Bulldogs athletic program, so unless you've got proof that I've done something against the law, back off."

Anderson swung his leg back into the car and balanced himself by holding the top of the door with his hand. "Get used to seeing me around. Until I'm convinced you aren't up to your neck in trouble, I'm going to be on you like stink on shit."

Anderson got into the driver's seat, slammed the door and backed out of the driveway. Driving away, he saw Joshua on the front porch, leaning against the door with his head in his hands.

Billings closed Chief McElroy's door as he left his office. Glancing over the crowded open cubicles, he made his way to the area he shared with Anderson. He found him with his face buried in a stack of files.

"Doug. You and I go back quite a few years."

Anderson continued reading, not even lifting his head when he answered. "Fifteen years and you know it. What's your point?"

Billings remained standing, rummaging through some books on the shelf across from their shared desk. "Do you ever regret staying in Athens and not taking the job in Atlanta with the DEA?"

Anderson slid his chair back away from the desk, his arms remaining flat on the desk top. He stared at his chewed nails with disinterest. "I don't even think about it anymore. What the hell brought that subject up?"

Billings continued to find things of interest on the bookshelf but remained silent.

Anderson repeated his question, this time a little more emphatic. "I said, why the fuck did you bring that up?"

Billings frowned at his partner's outburst. "Our relationship over the years has been a good one but lately things are getting a little strained. You and I operate with different philosophies. Always have, always will, but the gap between how we think has gotten much wider. We work together well and we respect each other, but your obsession over the murders of those drug dealers is creating a wedge between us and is driving the entire office staff nuts."

"Come on. You're getting a little deep with this." Anderson didn't realize how loudly he had spoken until he noticed the silence in the outer offices. When he looked up, several faces turned away. He blushed and nodded to those who were still staring.

"Sorry. I guess I am wound too tight. Has anyone in particular complained or is it just my sensitive partner?"

Billings took his seat. "I've just come from Chief McElroy's office. Does that give you a hint? He's a little pissed over your visit to the Smiths' home last night. He called me to his office and commanded me to rein you in before you fuck up and get suspended."

Anderson whistled and feigned gagging sounds.

Billings chuckled at his partner's antics but the grin on his face disappeared and his voice took on a more serious tone. "Let's talk about Joshua Smith. I know you've used up a lot of markers getting information on him. Why?"

Anderson sighed and collapsed in his chair. Interference from the top had begun.

CHAPTER 19

Doyle leaned back in his wicker chair, drawing deeply on a big cigar. He was content watching Carlos wash up the dinner dishes and place them in the dryer rack. After a couple of days together, they had become friends and shared every meal. They spent hours on the front stoop watching squirrels scamper through the large trees, performing acrobatic acts in the limbs. The conversations were sports-related with an occasional foray into hunting and fishing.

Carlos hung up the dish towel and dropped onto the small sofa across from Doyle. "I do the dishes anytime you cook for me. Where you learn to cook so good?"

Doyle pumped out his chest to show his pleasure over the compliment. "I spent a few years in the US Navy in my younger years. After I married Hazel, I thought my cooking days were over, but I didn't figure on her dying before me."

Carlos' voice softened. "What happened to her?"

Doyle developed a faraway stare. It was several moments before he returned his attention to Carlos. "Cancer took her. One month she was fine and the next month she was dead. Wasn't a long-drawn-out thing. She just got sicker by the day and one morning she didn't wake up. Once she found out she had cancer, she never went back to the doctor. I didn't try to talk her into it. I didn't blame her. I wouldn't want them cutting me up either. We always lived a simple life and we were happy with the time we had together. Not that I don't miss her. I miss her every day but I know she's okay where she is and it won't be long before I join her, although it's already been longer than I expected."

Carlos nodded his head, but remained silent.

Doyle blew out a puff of smoke. "What about you, Carlos? You don't talk about your life very much. I'm not the type to pry and you don't have to say a thing if you don't want to."

Carlos wasn't sure why, but for some reason he wanted to talk to this kind old man. "I guess you figured out that I not in the United States, legal. I hide, but not from Immigration. I run from bad trouble up in north Georgia. I no saint but some people up there think I do something bad. I think my brother-in-law set me up. He is bad. Only reason he not kill me is because I sell drugs for him and he needs me. I do not like to sell the drugs but if I not sell them, he will report me and he told me he would hurt my sister. I not want to go back there, but have to."

Doyle watched the smoke from his cigar curl upwards, disappearing in the wash of the revolving ceiling fan. "You don't have to. You can stay here for as long as you like. Immigration officers aren't likely to come around here and your bad 'friends' would have even a harder time locating you. I don't have much but I have a little pension and we can make do, at least until you find some place you'd rather be. I assume you don't want to go back to Mexico."

Carlos shook his head. "No. No family left in Mexico. My sister is the only family I have. Things very bad in Mexico. Not just for me. There is little work. When you work, you make only small money. My sister send me money to get across the border. Pete picked me up there. I felt I owe him, but he not treating me right."

Doyle pushed the cat from his lap and got up from his chair, motioning for Carlos to follow him. "I haven't told you the whole truth about my service days. In basic training I shot expert with the M-1, the M-14 and the M-16. Because of a special need, I was transferred to the Marines and was trained as a sniper. That was my MOS when I was sent to Vietnam. I spent two tours in Vietnam and most of my hunting was for two-legged animals. Can't say that I enjoyed it, but it was what my country asked me to do," he said.

"I managed to ship a lot of my favorite weapons home. Wasn't that hard to do if you knew the right people. I have one hell of a gun collection. Come on back to my bedroom and let me show you what I've acquired over the years."

The second week of Carlos' stay passed quickly and a strong bond developed between him and Doyle. The old man was a good listener and without prompting Carlos told him about his real problems and the fear of Pete, and the other drug dealers.

"It is bad to sell the drugs to the kids, but I have to do it or Pete will get me in a lot of trouble."

Doyle nodded and lifted his cane pole from the black water of the small river to check his bait. The shaded area under the large oaks was their favorite fishing hole and an excellent place for conversation.

"I didn't poison Timmy Smith," Carlos said. "I did what Pete told me to do. I think he is trying to get me in trouble with the other drug people so they will kill me and he will be rid of me. I have no way to fight him back."

"Carlos, you always have a choice in life. The question is whether or not you are willing to take risks. You've let your brother-in-law drive you into the illegal drug trade out of fear of being deported. If you go back, the situation will be the same, unless you are willing to do things to change it."

"What can I do? I'm just me. I have no power and no help up there."

Doyle glanced up at the sky where black clouds were boiling in from the west. He turned his attention back to Carlos. "Help is there. Sometimes you just have to look around and keep your eyes open to find it. Have you done much reading about the history of America?"

"I learn to read English very well but not study history books."

"Back in the Sixties and Seventies the United States got embroiled in a war in Vietnam. Obviously, the leaders of our country didn't read the history books either. They didn't learn from the mistakes made by the Japanese and the French. America tried to wage war with the Viet Cong using standard battle field tactics. It didn't work even though we had massive fire power, air superiority and logistics.

"Those little guys, the VC, lived out in the jungle and fought in small groups, sometimes only one or two people, but they were able to create havoc for much larger forces. Our troops were brave and good fighters but we didn't know the terrain. You've got to know how to make the area around you an ally. Hit 'em with surprise and the numbers won't matter," Doyle said.

"Just remember what I taught you about the guns and how to shoot. Don't get in a gun battle with them. Hit and leave. Let them fight shadows."

Carlos kept his eyes on Doyle's face and tried to look calmer than he felt, but did not speak.

"I know it's time for you to leave," Doyle said, "and I want you to take whatever you need with you. I don't want you to get hurt, but to have any kind of life; you've got to stand up for yourself."

Carlos knew it was time to go, as well, but he hated to leave his friend. The two weeks had gone fast and had been the happiest of his life. Were it not for his sister's situation, he would have stayed forever.

The silence between them was broken by a thunderclap, followed by rapid flashes of lightning. Heeding the warning signs, the two men gathered their equipment and headed home.

CHAPTER 20

Joshua parked his Jeep in the shadows cast by the light from a dim street lamp. For the hundredth time he questioned his sanity. Not only was he risking his football and academic career, he was also putting his life in danger. It would be a battle to evade discovery by the police while avoiding problems with the drug dealers. The former would lead to ruination of his future; the latter could cause his death.

Just as devastating would be the adverse effect on the UGA team at this critical time of the season. He wasn't concerned about the upcoming weekend game. The Bulldogs were heavily favored against a good Baylor team but one lacking in depth and one that would wilt in the Georgia sun. The following week would be the game against the hated Florida Gators. He would have to be at the top of his game to defeat the Gators. Better get this first cog in his plan over.

He climbed out and closed the door. He passed beneath a pole at the corner of the intersection, glancing up at the street signs to assure himself that he was at Hammond and Lee streets. His heart thumped against his sternum, matching the thunderous pulse in his temples. Cold sweat ran down his back but he fought back the panic and continued walking toward the boarded-up convenience store.

He murmured the instructions relayed to him by Rafael. "Come alone, stay in the center of the street until you reach the north wall of the building." Nothing more had been offered. He had no idea what he was to do after he got to that point.

Joshua swallowed the bile that arose in his throat, suppressing the urge to vomit. He hoped his trembling legs could not be seen by whoever lurked in the shadows. Reaching the edge of the building, he met the silence of a black void. He leaned against the brick wall, placing his hands in the front pockets of his jeans, more to hide the constant tremor than to look cool. His façade of calmness disappeared the moment he heard the deep rumbling voice from the shadows.

"Take yo' goddamn hands out of yo' pockets. Face the fucking wall and put yo' hands on the brick above yo' head and keep them there. You let yo' hands drop and I'll drop yo' sorry ass quick."

Joshua followed the orders, speaking over his shoulder. "Hey, what the shit, man. You think I'm carrying?"

"You better not be, asshole, or this will be yo' last night."

Joshua turned his head toward the voice, his eyes locking on the gun barrel aimed at his head. His eyes moved from the gun to the outstretched arm of the biggest, blackest man he had ever seen. With catlike quickness despite his bulk, the man placed himself behind Joshua and began to search him from his hair to his feet.

"Satisfied?" Joshua asked, the tremor in his voice betraying his bravado.

The massive black man slipped his gun in the waistband at the small of his back, then reached out with his left hand and spun Joshua around. "Can't be too careful in this business. My source told me you straight but I don't take any chances."

Joshua folded his arms across his chest, unsure what to do with his hands. He stared into the cold black eyes. "Your source was right. I'm not looking for trouble. I was told you had what I need and at the right price. Did your man tell you what I wanted and how much?"

A grin spread across the dealer's face revealing big yellow tobacco-stained teeth and blue gums. "Yeah. I got some problems with the quantity though—that's why you are seeing me. I don't let any of my dealers handle loads like you want. What's happening? You plan on starting yo' own business on my turf?"

"No way, man. I don't need to make money. My old man is loaded and gives me all the money I need. I've got a lot of friends who like to party, especially with the girls. You know how it is. They are a lot friendlier when they get happy."

The laugh came like a rumble from deep within a cave. "Oh! I see. You a pussy hound. That figures. Rich boys don't have nothing to do 'cept chase pussy and play with their toys."

Joshua flashed a smile, more at ease with the situation. "Well, do I get what I asked for?"

The man's grin disappeared, replaced by a scowl. "Maybe. Let me see the money, rich boy."

Joshua paused, and when he spoke his words were more daring than he felt. "Not yet. Do you have the stuff with you?"

A smile returned to the man's face, his large nostrils flaring as he spoke. "You show me the money, motherfucker, and the shit will be here within thirty seconds. If you ain't got the money, you better start running 'fore I waste yo' sorry white ass."

Joshua realized the moment of truth had arrived. He would complete the deal and get himself established with the dealer or he would be dying on the pavement, another victim of a drug deal gone bad. Moving with a deliberate motion to avoid spooking the dealer, he reached into his jacket and removed a large envelope.

"I've got two thousand in tens and twenties, just like I was told."

The dark man took the envelope, ripped it open and rapidly counted the money. Satisfied, he pocketed the money and in one swift move he had the gun out again and pointed at Joshua.

"You get five hundred worth tonight. The rest of the money will be like you have 'stablished some credit. I ain't crazy. No way I bring that much stuff with me on my first deal with you. I don't care who speak for you."

Joshua's face flushed, his neck veins distended. "Fuck you! Why didn't your gopher tell me this would be a limited deal? Shit, the risk is much greater for me. I sure ain't very comfortable walking around down here with this much cash on me."

The dealer sneered. "Tough shit, motherfucker. You play by our rules down here. You don't like it, get yo' white ass gone and don't come back—but how you goin' get in those little white girls' pants?"

The last remark riled Joshua even more, but not enough to screw up what he had accomplished. "I didn't say we needed it to get in their pants. It just makes it a lot quicker. Who wants to waste time working up some tail when you can do it in one night with a little 'help'?"

The dealer erupted in laughter, spraying spittle over Joshua's face. "Don't get your panties in a wad, kid. We can do business. Take what I give you. I don't hear no talk or have some cop on my ass, we do more business. You know how to reach me."

The dealer stuck the gun back in his waistband and retrieved a plastic bottle from his jacket pocket. "Five hundred worth of 'E.' All you get this trip. You straight, you get more, plus some of the hard stuff later, if you want it."

"I thought you said you didn't have anything with you."

The dealer laughed. "Until I see the cash, I don't have it with me. Get it? You better catch on to the rules fast, or you won't be making too many deals."

Joshua took the Ecstasy, squirreling it away inside his jacket. "I'll play by your rules. I just want to make sure I have a steady supplier. You ain't planning on going away, are you?"

"I be here. My source is good. I get any shit you want, long as you come up with the money. Just don't try to fuck me or I'll kill yo' ass. Understand, partner?"

Joshua relaxed a little for the first time since he approached the building. "I understand. What do I call you?"

"Manuel. All you need to know."

Joshua stared at the man. "You don't look Hispanic."

Manuel closed the gap between them in a flash, his hand reaching behind his back. "What the fuck to you what I am or called? Call me Hung Lo or Red Cloud if you want. I don't give a fuck, long as you got the money and don't fuck with me. Cops start sniffing 'round here, I come after yo' ass."

Joshua started to shout back but thought better of it. "I told you I'm straight. I just need a bigger supply. When can we meet again?"

Manuel was already retreating into the shadows but he answered, "Get in touch through our mutual friend. Just like this time. Let him know what you need. He tell you where we meet. Won't be here."

Joshua watched him disappear into the shadows, followed by sounds of several feet scuffing along the pavement. He realized he had been in the sights of a shooter the whole time he was with Manuel. He turned to leave but stopped when he heard a noise to his front.

He spun to his left, in the direction of the sound. Two men wearing hoods stepped from the shadows. The person closest to him slammed a fist into his gut. He doubled over and recovered in time to avoid a roundhouse that grazed his jaw. His victory was brief. A blow like a jackhammer pounded into his lower back sending him sprawling on the hard concrete surface.

A knee struck him higher on his back and an iron grip seized the back of his head, grinding his face into the rough pavement. He heard Manuel's voice.

"You're playing a man's game here, super jock. Make sure this is what you want before you come back. If you do come back, you better show some respect."

Joshua remained on the ground for several minutes after the noises retreated. He pushed up with his painful hands, getting to his feet. His legs trembled and his knees almost buckled before he regained control. As he walked back to his Jeep, mixed emotions surged through his body. He had never been this close to death before and things were not going to get any easier.

Somehow he would find the courage to do whatever was necessary, to deal with the scum, to place his life on the line; whatever was necessary to find a way to avenge Timmy's death.

CHAPTER 21

The huge scoreboard clock at the west end of Sanford Stadium revealed the story of the first half of the game between the hosting UGA Bulldogs and the Baylor Bears. Less than a minute remained. A majority of the players were leaning forward, their hands resting on the knees, as they struggled to recover from the heat and humidity.

Temperature in the mid-eighties, with ninety percent humidity, was siphoning the strength and fight from the losing team. This was a disturbing sight to the home team fans; it was their players who were gasping like fish out of water.

The Baylor Bears were in their offensive huddle on Georgia's ten-yard line, driving for another score before halftime. Even if the Bulldogs kept them out of the end zone, they were assured of at least a field goal and three additional points. A ten-point lead on the nationally ranked Bulldogs at halftime would send the Bears fans into frenzy and the Bulldog fans back to the concession stands for more beer.

Joshua stood on the sideline, his eyes focused on his shoes to avoid eye contact with his teammates and coaches. The anemic first thirty minutes of play was on his shoulders. His failure to move the offense resulted in the devastating fatigue that sapped the defensive players, since they were on the field for most of the first half.

The Baylor coaches had established a good game plan. Their team was grinding out the yardage on the ground and letting the clock work in their favor.

Unintentionally, Joshua's poor play was helping them and if he didn't improve, the coaches would pull him from the game. That wouldn't impress the pro scouts present at the game. He was projected to be a first-round draft pick in the upcoming NFL draft and being pulled for ineffectiveness against an unranked team would shoot that prospect down and cost him millions in bonus money.

When the official blew his whistle and the Baylor offensive team moved toward the line of scrimmage, Joshua held his breath. He needed the defense to hold them to three points. If he got his head back in the game, the team could rally in the second half and make up the deficit. Somehow he had to get his mind off the unnerving meeting with the drug dealer and back onto football.

The quarterback for Baylor barked out his signals. Taking the snap, he faked to the fullback in the middle, tucked the ball under his right arm and followed the halfback in a sweep around his right end. The running back took out the outside linebacker and the path looked open to the end zone but the strong safety leaped over his fallen teammate and made a tremendous tackle, dropping the QB at the half yard line. The defense had held but Baylor had a partial victory.

The play had resulted in perfect positioning of the football for their left-footed kicker. Another snap, a cheer from the visitors clustered together in the end zone seats, and Baylor had their ten-point lead. Not overwhelming against a team like the Bulldogs, but surprising none the less.

Joshua picked up his helmet from the bench, joining the other players jogging toward the dressing room.

The quarterback coach grabbed his arm, halting his progress. "Smith, wait for me inside the building. Don't enter the dressing room. I'll be along in a few minutes."

Joshua ran to catch up with his teammates. Looking back over his shoulder, he saw the QB coach conferring with the head coach. Joshua could already feel the hook. Worse yet, near the entrance to the tunnel leading to the dressing room, he saw his father and the disappointment on his face. Joshua thought he knew what his father was thinking. First, he loses a son to drugs, and now his other son, who is supposed to be a star athlete, is stinking up the place.

The few minutes until the assistant coaches arrived seemed like hours to Joshua. Each of the coaches made eye contact with him and a couple of them spoke words of encouragement, but none of them stopped.

The door opened again and the offensive coordinator and the QB coach walked in together, involved in a heated discussion. Joshua knew he was the topic of the discussion.

The two men separated, with the coordinator continuing on while the quarterback coach stopped at Joshua's side. He looked into Joshua's eyes with a no-nonsense expression on his face. "Smith, you are playing way below your ability. Is there something I need to know? Do you have an injury that hasn't been reported to the trainer?"

Joshua wished he had a legitimate injury to use as an excuse. "I feel fine, coach. I just can't stay focused on the plays."

"I would have understood if you played this bad three weeks ago after your brother died, but you had a fantastic game against Arkansas even after being out of practice for a week and missing the Western Carolina game," the coach said. "I was sure you had buried your grief for the good of the team, but now I'm not so sure. Your inability to focus, as you put it, is a little self-centered and a result of your own pity party."

Joshua wanted to look away but he met the coach's eyes unflinchingly.

"Get it together or I'll pull you in the second half," the coach said. "Franklin isn't the athlete that you are, but when on, he can get the job done. If you keep playing like you did in the first half, you won't get the job done, and the game next week against the Gators won't matter very much."

The reference to the run at the SEC Championship, which required that the Bulldogs defeat Florida and the Auburn Tigers, got Joshua's attention.

He knew the coach wanted it for the team and not just for himself. "I can get the job done, coach. I've got problems in my personal life and I let it interfere, but I promise to get my act together and I won't let the team down."

The coach gave him a pat on the shoulder, and pushed him toward the remainder of the team gathered around the head coach. "I know you can, Joshua. Your teammates know it, too. Let's go see what they have drawn up for the second half."

Approaching the other players, Joshua thought about what had just taken place. That was the first time the coach had called him by his first name since he had visited the Smiths' home on a recruitment trip. With such a simple act, the coach made him realize the coaching staff was there with him, even though they appeared to be distant.

The UGA Bulldogs awakened in the second half, scoring thirty-four unanswered points. Joshua passed for over two hundred yards and four touchdowns in a quarter and a half, before turning it over to his backup. The fans were delirious, the pro scouts were impressed and the coaches had their star athlete back in the fold.

CHAPTER 22

The gray overcast did little to help Detective Anderson's mood as he climbed the granite steps at police headquarters. He suppressed his crappy mood long enough to carry on some friendly banter with two patrolmen just beginning their daily rounds. It wasn't that long ago that his days started in a similar manner. Now he was supposed to enjoy the fruits of his labor in his cushy detective job, but things were not always what they seemed.

Truth be known, he envied the patrolmen even though their job was a mixture of the mundane and sudden terror. When things were peaceful, it was a great job, enjoying the freedom of moving around the city, seeing friends on street corners and in shops. The beat cops enjoyed the admiration of the school kids, at least the elementary age group. By the time the kids reached middle school age, they either had a healthy respect for the cops or despised them, based on the attitude of their parents and neighborhood friends. Admired or hated, the cops still did their jobs in spite of the low pay and long hours.

The job took its toll on many marriages and some young men who started out with patriotic fervor soured on the public and became prey for those who knew how to take advantage of such situations.

Aware of those possibilities, Anderson took the time to offer encouragement to the young patrolmen, urging them to continue to serve even if their efforts were not always recognized.

Entering his office, Anderson found Billings smiling like Sylvester the Cat, right after he swallowed Tweety Bird. Anderson was determined to ignore Billings, not giving him the opportunity to start the "guess what I know" game. He didn't want to be at the office today, much less play Billings' silly game, but it would have been hypocritical for him to say so, after his pep talk with the men downstairs.

Billings caved in first. "Guess what?"

"Come on, Marvin. I'm in a shitty mood today. Don't start on me."

Billings' expression revealed his disappointment. "Spoil sport." The smile returned. "Carlos is back in town. A couple of my informants spotted him and called me. He's at the usual hangouts."

Anderson got up from his chair, leaving the stack of files on his desk untouched. "Well, I guess we need to pay Carlos a visit and find out where he's been. Anything you need before we go?"

Billings grabbed his jacket draped over the coat rack. "Nothing important enough to keep me from my appointed rounds."

Opening the door for his partner, Anderson quipped, "I hate to inform you, partner, but that's a saying from the US Postal Service. Detectives don't have memorable slogans."

"Other than the weather, nothing changes around here," Carlos remarked to himself. "Gone for two weeks, come back to the same street corners and nobody blinks."

Not a single customer had commented on his absence. They just sidled up to him, made small talk, got what they wanted, and cut out.

It was almost time for classes to end so Carlos moved south on Baxter Street toward Milledge Avenue. A lot of the students would be returning to the fraternity and sorority houses. They would expect to find him, or his stand-in, walking along Milledge, making it easy for quick buys.

Carlos saw the beige sedan approaching on his side of the street and he crossed to the other side. His maneuver didn't work. The driver swung the car into a quick U-turn and pulled alongside.

Billings jumped out, opened the back door, motioning for Carlos to get in. "Let's go for a ride, Carlos."

Carlos balked. "Why you hassle me? I'm just walking to the store."

"Fucking A," Anderson yelled at him. "You live over ten miles from here. What's the matter, grocery prices too high in your neighborhood?"

Billings stuck his head back into the car. "Let me handle this."

An Athenian behind them grew impatient and began to lean on his car horn. Billings held up his badge, waved him around their car and then turned back to Carlos.

"Get in the damn car. We just want to ask you some questions, but if you fuck with us, I'll radio for a black-and-white and have you arrested for jaywalking. I'm sure a routine pat-down will be productive."

Carlos paused for a second to consider his options. Deciding there were none, he crawled into the back seat of the sedan.

The detectives remained silent until they reached the parking lot of the University library. Anderson switched off the ignition and looked back over his shoulder at Carlos. "Been on a trip?"

Carlos shrugged his shoulders. "I went to Vegas. Somebody told me Elvis was back."

Anderson's face reddened. "I'd say the timing was good for a vacation but I doubt you found Elvis." Changing tactics, he shouted, "Tell me about the Smith kid."

Carlos squirmed in the seat. "You guys know what I do, but I never hurt anybody. I liked Timmy. I never do anything to hurt him."

Billings took over. "Well, somebody did. The crime lab report indicated there was enough strychnine in that cocaine you sold him, to kill several people. That was no cut job. Somebody intentionally poisoned him. No other cases have been reported, so what you sold him was the only tainted stuff out there."

Carlos began to sweat. "I just do what the big people tell me to do. They said it was a present to Timmy for being such a good customer. I think nothing about it at the time, until I heard he died. It made me sick. I liked him."

Anderson jumped in. "Why did someone want to hurt him? Who was it? Did they have a problem with the kid or did they have something against Dr. Smith, his father?"

Carlos took a handkerchief from his pocket and wiped the sweat from his forehead and eyes, then shook his head. "I never heard them talk about him. They not talk to me about business. They just tell me, 'Do this or do that.' Manuel threatened to kill me, like it was my fault. So I ran."

Anderson made eye contact with Billings. They both picked up on the mention of someone named Manuel.

"Tell you what, Carlos. Work with us on this and if what you say is true, I can promise you'll not get charged with the kid's death," Anderson said.

"What about what I do—you know—selling the drugs? If I get charged, they send me back to Mexico."

"I can't make any promises on that, but we'll do all we can. We got a deal?"

They waited in silence except for Carlos' heavy breathing. Finally, he muttered, "Deal."

Billings opened the back door. He watched Carlos walk away and gave him a parting shot. "Don't plan on any more vacations right away.

If Elvis does come back, it'll be to Memphis."

Carlos stopped in his tracks and turned back to face him. "Do not hassle me. I get into trouble if I am picked up too often."

Billings backed into the car, grabbed the door handle, but stopped the movement of the door. "We'll pass the word to let you be for awhile, but you had better come through for us. If you disappear again, we'll call the Feds and your picture will be on CNN before you can get out of Athens."

CHAPTER 23

A mass of black clouds rolled through the afternoon sky, accompanied by sudden gusts of wind that sent small whirlwinds of dead oak leaves across the parking lot of the Athens Country Club.

Joshua sat in his Jeep watching golfers race the oncoming storm, driving their golf carts to their limits, to reach the safety of the underground storage. Lightning flashed across the sky, from cloud to cloud, followed by a bolt from cloud to ground. Before the following thunderous clap finished, heavy sheets of rain fell from the sodden sky. Several of the players who prolonged their playing time too long were getting drenched in sight of the club house, and yet were too far to turn back to the shelters built in the middle of the course.

The Jeep rocked in the wind gusts. Small branches and acorns blown from the massive oak trees bombarded the roof top like small missiles. The storm, which arrived with sudden furor, quickly dissipated, leaving the course and parking lot littered with leaves, twigs and paper. Joshua saw Ed Hoard, the head pro, standing on the covered veranda surveying the damage.

Watching Hoard, Joshua failed to see the man who approached the Jeep. Startled, he jerked upright when the passenger door opened.

Pete Dawson slid into the opposite seat. He was soaked, with heavy streams of water flowing from his thin hair down across his face and onto the floor. He wiped his hands across his face. "Damn, for a second, I thought my ass was fried."

Joshua reached into the back seat for his locker bag and extracted a towel. "Sorry, the towel isn't clean, but it's all I got."

The man accepted the towel, and began to wipe his head and face. The towel was useless for his soaked clothes.

"Who the hell are you?" Joshua asked.

"I work with Manuel. I'm Pete." He offered his hand, which Joshua ignored.

"Where did you park?"

"About three hundred yards from here, on a road alongside the railroad tracks. I saw your Jeep from the highway, but decided not to drive my car onto the property. I walked through the service gate figuring I had plenty of time to get here before the rain, but it caught me about halfway."

Joshua nodded. "There was a message taped to my steering wheel to be here at six o'clock. I expected to be meeting Manuel. What's the deal?"

Pete unzipped his jacket, extracting a soggy envelope from an inside pocket. "I'm just a messenger. Manuel told me to deliver this to you, personally. Otherwise I would have left it in your Jeep, instead of the note."

Joshua opened the envelope, removed a single sheet of paper and glanced over the words. Folding the note, he placed it in his shirt pocket.

Pete sat in silence for a moment. "Need me to take anything back to Manuel?"

"No. It was just some information I requested from Manuel." Joshua recognized Pete's fishing attempt, but kept the information to himself.

"How about dropping me by my car?" Pete asked. "These wet jeans are chafing my ass."

Cranking the Jeep, Joshua drove toward the large black iron gate. "Next time, pick a less conspicuous place. Too many people know me around here and might wonder why I'm meeting someone in the parking lot."

After dropping Pete at his car, Joshua drove back into Athens. He wondered what Manuel was up to, and why he had changed their usual place and time for their meeting.

Joshua drove along US Highway 129, the two-lane blacktop that connected the cities of Athens and Jefferson, passing through a sparsely populated area of northeast Georgia. Large expanses of pasture held rolls of hay scattered around the fields like sentinels, guarding clusters of cattle and goats.

Approaching the small town of Arcade, halfway between the cities, he reviewed the instructions in Manuel's note. Slowing to twenty-five miles an hour, he began to reconnoiter each side of the highway. At exactly a quarter mile inside the city limit sign, he saw the turnoff, near the small antique shop mentioned in the note. He swung the Jeep left onto the secondary road and increased his speed. Four and eight-tenths miles from the turnoff, he found a dirt road adjacent to a large sweet gum tree. He drove down the rough road for one mile, stopped the Jeep, switched off the ignition and waited.

Ten minutes passed, then twenty; the area remained deserted. Joshua wiped his sweaty hands on the front of his jeans. Fidgeting in his seat, he remembered the times in earlier years when he had yelled at Timmy for being so impatient while standing in line at Six Flags. He checked the rear view mirror again, willing Manuel to appear.

Reaching his limit of patience, he climbed out of the vehicle and stood at the front, leaning back on the hood. He heard rushing water nearby but didn't see a stream or river; however, he did remember passing a small lake just before turning on to the dirt road. He watched a crow fly across the sky, fending off a small sparrow diving like a fighter plane at the big black bird.

Infuriated by the wait, he circled his Jeep, staring back at the way he had come. He neither saw nor heard any vehicles on the dirt road or the secondary road. The area around him was covered with weeds and brush, with a few decayed beer cans lying near the road. He began to sweat again, his heart pounding. He realized he was a fool for standing here as a target for one of Manuel's goons.

A deep roar echoed from the direction of the highway. The sound was muffled for a moment before it became louder again. Joshua faced the direction of the noise and saw a motorcycle, with a single rider astride, maneuvering through the deep ruts of the dirt road. The rider, decked out in a black leather jacket, was also wearing a black helmet with a dark visor, making identification impossible. The black and silver Harley slowed, approached cautiously, and stopped alongside the Jeep.

Joshua looked past the rider, but he saw no one else. Unnerved, Joshua imagined sounds from the woods around him, but refused to turn his head to look. Instead, he stood his ground, waiting on the biker to dismount.

Manuel pushed back the visor, removed his helmet, and hung it on the handlebars. He ran his gloved fingers through his hair, dismounted from the bike and stretched. Removing his gloves, he finally spoke. "Good to see you, kid. Obviously, you got my message."

Joshua snapped. "What's with the big mystery? Why in hell are we meeting out here? You pissed with me? You plan to let your goons waste me and dump me out here? And what happened to your 'gangbanger' slang?"

"Hey! Fuck you, kid. I have my damn reasons. If you want to deal with me in the future, shut your yap and listen. You got eyes. I came alone."

"That's what you say, but I think you have backup scattered out in the woods. I heard noises back in the trees. Hell, you told me before that you have your reasons for caution."

Manuel slammed his gloves on the seat of the big bike. "I told you, I'm alone. I have my reasons for meeting out here. You haven't been truthful with me, amigo."

Joshua swallowed hard, his mouth like cotton. "What the hell are you talking about?"

A smirk appeared on Manuel's face. He spat his words at Joshua. "I'm talking about you telling me you weren't selling. Word I get, you are the main source for half the football team."

Relief swept over Joshua. This accusation he could handle, as long as Manuel didn't know of his true involvement. "That's a bunch of crap. I'm not selling to anybody. I don't need the money. I don't use drugs, and I have no reason to suspect any of the players. We are watched too closely to take that chance. The girls are a different matter—they don't have to worry about losing a scholarship."

"Don't be a smart ass, kid. You're Doc Smith's brat. How would your daddy feel about his boy being involved in drugs, especially since he's lost one boy already?"

Joshua's face reddened, his nostrils flaring at the mention of Timmy's death, by this scum. He suppressed his anger, unwilling to allow Manuel to goad him into blowing his cover. "I'm sure he wouldn't believe it, no matter who told him. He would be certain I wouldn't jeopardize my position on the team. As long as he believes that, I'm safe. Have you decided you don't like the money you're making on these deals?"

"Easy now. I didn't say I was going to tell your old man. I'm just fucking with you. I'm just surprised you are into drugs after what happened to your little brother."

Joshua leaned against the Jeep. "We all have our reasons. Just remember I'm not in competition with you."

Manuel stepped away from the bike, walked to the back of the Jeep, and propped his foot on the bumper. Brushing pine needles from his boot, he said, "You are so high and mighty. You too good to use the stuff, but you get it for your friends. I remember, you're a super-jock, a real tough guy."

Joshua straightened, widening his stance, his arms dropped to his side, his fists clenched. "It's clear I'm a lot tougher than you. I come to all these meetings alone, while you always have two or three guys with you."

Manuel sniffed hard and spat at Joshua's feet. "I told you, I'm alone and I don't need any help handling you or any other snotty-nose rich kid like you. I have those people around when I got big money or a lot of drugs on me."

"Well, if you don't have backup today, obviously you don't have money or drugs, so why the hell did you get me out here—just to tell me you know my father is a doctor?"

The man grinned. "I've got another proposition for you. It doesn't involve drugs, but it can make me a lot of money I don't have to pass up the line, if you get my drift."

"Well, are you going to tell me, or stand there smiling like an idiot?"

Manuel took a step toward Joshua. "Watch it, kid. I may be alone, but I can hurt your ass if I get a mind to. Your mommy might just go off the deep end if she loses another kid."

Joshua slipped his hand into his jacket pocket and gripped the handle of the Glock. The tension of the moment was pushing things out of his control, and at risk to his own plans, he would shoot Manuel in the face if he stepped any closer.

"Goddamn kid," Manuel said. "You are touchy today. If we are going to do business, we got to have a better understanding."

Joshua released the handle of the gun, but kept his hand in the jacket pocket. "Okay. What's this deal you want to tell me about and how do I figure in?"

Manuel clapped his hands together suddenly. "You are the main cog in this deal. You've got three games left in the regular season and two of them are against SEC opponents. Those two games will have point spreads less than four points. You keep the score in a range that I dictate to you and I'll make a fortune with the bookies. That will give me a nice nest egg to start my own business."

Joshua's initial thoughts were to tell this low-life to go to hell. He refused to fix games for anybody, no matter what the reward, but he swallowed his anger to learn more of Manuel's plans. "What about the post-season games? If we win out in the regular season, there's a good chance we'll be in a major BCS game, maybe for the national championship."

"I like your thinking, but let's take this one step at a time. We can't afford to get greedy."

Joshua used the opportunity to fish for more information on the drug operations. "You figure the people who own you are going to let you move in on their turf?"

"Nobody owns Manuel. I work for the *man* but when I get ready to cut out, ain't nobody going to stop me."

Joshua backed off, playing along to learn more. "You know sometimes it's impossible to control the flow of a game. I might be able to control our offensive production but I can't do a damn thing about defensive points."

"Don't worry about specifics. Just make sure Georgia loses to Florida. One point or fifty, I don't care. Just make sure they lose. We'll take the others game by game and I'll tell you before each game what leeway you got."

With a spurious smile on his face, Joshua stuck out his hand, and Manuel shook it. "Okay, Manuel. I think we can work together. I don't have time to drive out here every time you want to meet, and I can't be seen with you or some reporter might get inquisitive and start asking questions."

Manuel nodded. "I've got a place just outside Athens. Up to now, there was no need for you to know about it, but since we are going to be partners, I'll give you directions. Just make sure no else knows about it or ever comes with you."

"I got it."

"Let me get a pen and I'll draw you a map."

While Manuel dug in the saddle bags for a pen and paper, Joshua scanned the woods for the source of the noise.

PJ sat in her car, both hands gripping the top of the steering wheel, her forehead resting on them. She was parked directly in front of the Smith home. It had not been her destination when she left the sorority house. Her plans were to drive to Georgia Mall just to window shop to clear her mind of the recent events. She drove instead through the various subdivisions and, as if the car had a will of its own, she found herself parked in Joshua's driveway.

She blotted her tears with the cuffs of her blouse and switched off the engine. When she opened the door to get out she had no plan as to who she would see or what she would do. Fate took care of that when Constance Smith opened the door before PJ knocked.

"PJ. How nice for you to visit me. I don't get out much and not many of my friends call on me. I think James has scared them off. He thinks I'm a basket case. He's probably right but still…"

"Mrs. Smith, I hope I'm not interrupting you. I should have called but I happened to be in the neighborhood and thought I would drop by. You look lovely in that dressing gown and jacket."

"Come in, honey, and let me remind you again to call me Connie—well at least until you can officially call me 'Mother.' And don't start our visit by lying about my appearance. I look like a washed-out hag and I know it. I rarely get out of my sleeping apparel but I'm making an effort. Please join me in the kitchen for coffee."

The two women walked to the kitchen where PJ motioned for Connie to sit while she filled two cups from a freshly brewed pot on the counter. She noticed that cream and sugar were already on the table.

"Connie—I like the sound of that, it makes me feel closer to you. I shouldn't have dropped in like this. I respect what you are going through and I know you need your privacy, but…"

"Joshua?" Connie asked.

"Yes. He's acting so strange. It's not grief reaction. He's apparently accepted Timmy's death and has moved on."

"Unlike some of us who can't."

"I'm sorry. I didn't mean to imply anything. I know I haven't done as well as Joshua, and I can't begin to imagine the pain that you feel."

PJ saw tears fill Connie's eyes and she quickly moved on. "Something more sinister has claimed Joshua. He's preoccupied all the time with things he refuses to discuss with me. It has affected his performance on the field and in the classroom."

"Honey, you might as well learn right now that men don't tell their women everything. It's part of that 'women are too weak and can't handle it' mentality they have. I've experienced the same thing with James for over four years, starting soon after his first medical missionary trips to South America." She looked down at her coffee cup.

"I learned a long time ago not to pressure him about things he doesn't wish to discuss. I'm not the snooping housewife type but I have my suspicions as to what's going on. Forgive me if I don't divulge them. It's not that I don't trust you—it's just something that's best left unsaid."

PJ's face blanched as she heard the words. First, Timmy's suspicions and now his mother's. Please God, she silently prayed, please don't let Joshua be involved as well.

She saw Connie take a sip of her coffee, replace the cup on the saucer and push it away. The signal that the visit was over. Maybe she was tired but most likely the conversation had entered areas that Connie had shut out of her mind and would not pursue.

She slid back her chair, moved around behind Connie and kissed her on the cheek. "I'll show myself out. Please enjoy your coffee and solitude. I promise to visit again soon."

As PJ walked down the steps toward her car, her mind was reeling and her heart heavy from knowledge that her precious Joshua might be involved in something that could take him from her forever.

CHAPTER 24

Detective Anderson ran his hand over his close-cropped hair in a gesture of frustration. The files of murdered drug dealers were getting more numerous each month, none of the cases even close to resolution.

"Marvin, what are we overlooking? We've spent more time on these murders than anything I can remember, yet our investigations create more questions than answers."

Anderson opened a desk drawer searching for Tylenol. His search unsuccessful, he slammed the drawer shut. A small individual packet of Tylenol Extra Strength landed on his desk and he thanked his benefactor without looking up. "Thanks. I'm getting a killer headache reading these damn files. The more I read, the more confused I become."

"Partner, you can read that stack of paper until the print comes off, but unless we get lucky, we ain't solving anything. These perps know how to cover their tracks. We're not fooling with amateurs."

Anderson popped the caplets in his mouth, washing them down with a swallow of cold coffee. "Are we missing signs of a turf takeover? I know we've hashed that over before, but why else would so many dealers get wasted in such a short time?"

Billings paused, considering the question. "I can't say for certain. I've talked with friends in other cities and all of them agree on one thing; if there's a turf battle or a takeover, new faces start showing up. If either the Asians or the Hispanics move in on the blacks, they make their presence known and leave a clear message the old crowd is no longer in charge."

Anderson leaned back in his chair, his hands behind his head. His partner's words bounced around in his brain. "Why aren't we seeing new people? I bet those fuckers are as confused as we are. Maybe we need to get someone from out of our city to infiltrate the local bunch."

"Not a bad idea if we can get the chief to okay it. He'll scream budget restraints but I think he'll buy in on it. Thing is, it will take months before our man would be effective."

"That won't help us. Maybe we can get someone on the inside to turn. If we offer enough inducement, it might be possible. The media is getting worked up over this and it won't be long before the commissioners will be all over the chief's ass."

A smile crossed Billings' face. "Now, that might be an interesting thing to see."

"You think so."

"No, I'm fooling, man. We both know that shit flows downhill. If he catches it from the commissioners, we will be up to our necks in a cesspool."

CHAPTER 25

The crowd in Bishop Park was large for a late fall evening in the middle of the week. Several soccer matches were in action on the divided fields. Children ran helter-skelter between temporary goals to the cheers of adoring parents who surrounded the playing fields.

Carlos considered the hectic activity ideal for his meeting with Joshua. He had listened to Eddie's pleas to meet with Joshua for several days, but was reluctant to meet in any location, fearing retaliation for Timmy's death. Joshua didn't know of Carlos' innocence. It had taken several hours of repeated reassurance that Joshua only wanted information, before Carlos agreed to the meeting.

Joshua waited in his Jeep on a hill overlooking the park. He was concerned as well, but for a different reason. He felt the place too exposed and being a local sports celebrity, he was concerned someone would recognize him while meeting with Carlos.

Joshua identified Carlos by the red shirt and white bandana he was wearing, as instructed by Eddie. Likewise, Joshua was to wear a light blue Polo shirt and a dark blue sweater draped around his neck.

The two men met at a fence separating the fields. Introductions were unnecessary and handshakes weren't expected. After warily checking the people around them, they looked each other over. It was obvious to Joshua that the other man was as uneasy over the meeting as he was.

"I know you are aware I'm Timmy's brother," he said. "Anything else you know about me is not important. I'm not here to create trouble for you. I have more to lose than you."

Carlos wiped his hands repeatedly on his pants as he glanced around them. "We both can lose a lot—our lives. These people you want to know about are bad hombres. They kill us if they know we talk."

A trickle of sweat rolled down Joshua's back even though it was a cool day. Doubt over his quest crept into his mind once again. He had always taken the safe road, avoiding situations that would damage his reputation or career. Those days of self-serving decisions were over.

"That's a risk I have to take. I need to know more about the people who control you. The ones you fear."

Carlos spat in the dirt at his feet. "I no say I afraid of them. I just know what can happen."

Realizing his mistake, Joshua backed off his rhetoric and chose a different path. "From what Eddie told me about you, I believe him when he says you had nothing to do with Timmy's death."

Carlos spoke in a whisper. "That is so. I liked Timmy. We were not friends, like him and Eddie, but we got along and he always nice to me. I would not hurt him. Some people make things bad for me. I tell you more about me... you will agree."

The tension between the two men dissipated and a handshake broke the ice. "My Jeep is parked up on the hill near those trees. It's identical to the one Timmy drove. I'll pick you up at the entrance to the park. We need to get away from all these people. I have a lot to ask you and I hope you have the answers."

Carlos hesitated. "Where do we go?"

"I know a place near the north branch of the Oconee River. It's not far and few people go there during the week. We can take our time and unload on each other."

Carlos looked as though he was unsure what the phrase meant, but he agreed.

They rode in silence for the fifteen minutes it took to reach the secluded spot. The north branch of the Oconee River was not a large river and at the site Joshua selected, it was wide and shallow with multiple sand bars jutting out from the banks. The shallow waters and the gentle flow made it a popular summer location for families with small children. During fall and winter months it was used less, with the exception of occasional fraternity blowouts. Just beyond the park the river narrowed as it coursed over large rocks, creating a cool, soothing sound.

Joshua sat on top of a picnic table with his feet resting on the concrete seat. He motioned for Carlos to join him. "I have little experience in the use of drugs. I've never used them or bought any, until I started my recent efforts."

The small Hispanic kept his eyes down, watching an ant crawl across the top of his worn-out running shoes. Joshua could see the tension in the man's body and waited to see if Carlos would decide to trust him.

The man took a deep breath and said, "Okay. I help you."

Joshua grabbed Carlos by the shoulders. "That's great. Let's get started."

The thing that puzzled Joshua for so long was solved, when Carlos told him that Timmy hadn't ordered the cocaine; it had been a "gift" from Pete.

Carlos returned to the streets in his usual spots. He made a few drops and, as instructed by Joshua, relayed a message to Manuel that Joshua needed to make a large purchase immediately.

Joshua slid behind the wheel of a Toyota Camry, borrowed from a friend. The tire wells were a collection of rust, and dents were more prevalent than flat surfaces, but the car was perfect for his purpose. His Jeep was too recognizable and his teammate, Mark Ashton, was more than willing to trade for the evening.

Traffic on the Athens Bypass was less congested than usual, allowing Joshua to reach the Danielsville exit much sooner than anticipated. Turning onto the four-lane asphalt road, he noted the odometer reading. The note left by Carlos instructed him to drive exactly eight and two-tenths miles, locate the billboard advertising Diet Coke, and turn at the next blacktop road on the right.

Light from a half moon made it easy to follow the directions after he turned off the highway. Four-tenths of a mile from the turnoff, he saw a black Ford Mustang parked facing toward him. He passed the car, noting a single occupant in the driver's seat. After another half mile he turned toward a pasture gate, reversed back onto the county road and drove up behind the lone car. Still following his instructions, he got out of the car and waited.

Several agonizing minutes passed before the door of the Mustang opened. A stocky, square-faced white male climbed out. It was not Manuel.

Joshua stiffened and considered jumping back into his car and hauling ass, but decided to play out the situation. He was confident the person walking in his direction was not a narcotic agent, and it was unlikely Carlos would have set him up. This was some low-life doing Manuel's leg work.

The man walked to within ten feet of Joshua before he spoke. "You got business on my road?"

Joshua recognized the identifying phrase and relaxed. He released his grip on the handle of his Glock and removed his hand from his jacket pocket. "Depends on the business."

The stranger walked closer, stopped and propped against the front fender of the Camry. "You look a little spooked. Who did you expect to find?"

"Manuel."

When the man reached into his coat pocket, Joshua tensed up, and in response grasped the handle of his gun. He fought the urge to pull out his weapon, exhaling in relief when the man pulled out a small cigar.

"I'm doing Manuel's business tonight. You got a problem with that?"

"Not if the price is the same and the stuff is good and hasn't been cut."

The man peered out from beneath his cap, turning his head at an angle studying Joshua. "Hey, I think I know you."

Joshua stood a little straighter, his senses alert to an apparent threat. "I doubt it. I just moved here from Florida. Things got too hot in Miami. I like these college towns better. Didn't Manuel tell you who to expect?"

"He said something, but I forgot."

"You got what I want?"

The dealer removed the cigar from his mouth, motioning for Joshua to follow him to the other car. "I got what Manuel sent. He read your note and saw no problem with your request. You got the money?"

Joshua removed a foil-wrapped packet from inside his jacket, passing it to the dealer.

Without opening the packet, the dealer stuck it in his coat pocket, popped the trunk lid and removed a small box, which he passed to Joshua.

"Aren't you going to count the money?"

"No need, my friend. If it ain't all there, I'm sure Manuel will look you up."

Joshua backed away from the Mustang and turned toward his car. "Nice doing business with a professional. Maybe I'll see you again in the future."

The man smiled. "Maybe."

As instructed, Joshua left first—an added precaution so he couldn't follow the dealer. It didn't matter to him. His mind was on Manuel.

Why had he ducked out on their planned meeting?

The dealer watched the Camry's tail lights disappear. He stared after the car for several moments before things clicked. "From Florida, my ass," he said to himself. "Joshua Smith, number one quarterback for the 'Dogs.' What in the hell are you doing in the drug business? Now that's a nice piece of information to know."

He removed a small pistol from his coat pocket and placed it under his seat. He reached for the ignition key, hesitating when he heard a sound outside his window. He turned toward the sound and saw a bright flash. He didn't feel the soft-nose bullet crash through his brain.

CHAPTER 26

Eddie stood outside the dorm for the university athletes. He felt butterflies in his stomach over the scheduled meeting with Joshua. It had been days since they last talked, because Joshua was wrapped up in preparation for the Florida game.

Eddie was eager to see inside the building, as most high school kids would be, but he wished it was under different circumstances. The message left on his cell phone, a gift from Joshua, had been curt and to the point, so he left school early to be at the dorm on time.

Joshua opened the door to his room as soon as Eddie knocked. He grinned when he saw the look on Eddie's face. "I was looking out the window and saw you standing in front of the dorm. You took so long getting to my room, I thought you were lost."

Eddie gave a half-hearted laugh and followed him into the room. He glanced around, surprised at the absence of sports posters or pinups. The room was spartan, but comfortable, with ample space for books adjacent to the desks. It looked like a room belonging to a nerd, rather than a star athlete.

Joshua sat at his desk and closed the English lit book. He motioned for Eddie to sit on the edge of his bed. "How many people have you told about our plans?"

Eddie looked surprised at the question. "Just Calvin—remember, I told you about Calvin. He knows a lot about drug busts and shit like that from listening to his dad. Am I not doing things right? Do you not trust me?"

Joshua rubbed his eyes. "I'm not questioning your actions. I agree Calvin is a good resource, but let's keep it to the three of us. I haven't told PJ and don't plan to tell her. The more people involved, the greater the risk something will slip in a conversation and we'll have big problems—the least of which would be from the police."

Eddie nodded in agreement.

Joshua turned away, closing his eyes for a second as he rubbed his forehead. His mind and heart were engaged in perpetual warfare that began when he and Eddie developed their first plan. He could deal with his involvement, whatever the consequences, but he could not justify to his conscience, the potential harm to his friends, especially Eddie, Calvin and PJ. The adverse publicity would also affect his parents and the University. Maybe the ends justified the means, he thought, but no one would know for sure until the heat was on.

He recalled how he felt when he read the news story in the *Athens Banner-Herald* about the deaths of the other dealers. He felt no remorse. He felt nothing, neither satisfaction or revenge or sorrow over the loss of a human life. The emptiness in his heart made him question his goals and whether his actions would change him as a human being.

Now he was unsure if he or the others could handle the mental stress involved. If the police learned of his involvement, he would be a prime suspect in the mysterious deaths, in spite of the fact he had harmed no one.

"Still with me, big guy?" Eddie chuckled. "Looks like you drifted off into space but I know you weren't thinking about PJ, because you aren't smiling."

Joshua responded with an attempt at a smile. "Sorry, Eddie. I get so wrapped up in the details, I forget where I am."

"I know how you feel. I do the same, sometimes. It's pretty scary what's happening to all the drug dealers. Carlos told me that his brother-in-law, Pete, won't even leave his house unless his boss makes him. Well, maybe we'll get a chance to question Pete."

Joshua looked up, his eyes locked on Eddie. Was this a fishing expedition? Eddie didn't know the details of his dealing with Manuel, but he thought Eddie had suspicions he never vocalized. Eddie and Calvin knew he wanted Manuel and all the other scumbags to die, but he would never admit any involvement to them. The less they knew, the more protected they would be.

When Joshua didn't respond to the last remark, Eddie asked, "Are you ready for me to contact Carlos and set up a meeting with Pete?"

"No. I've got an exam in English lit tomorrow, and I've got to get ready to travel to Jacksonville to play the game against the Gators. It will be a Saturday night game so we won't be back until Sunday afternoon. If everything is okay at that time, we'll meet and discuss the arrangements for a meeting with Pete. That's why I wanted to see you."

"I want you to take it easy this weekend," Joshua said. "Be sure and watch the game on TV. Florida has a great passing quarterback and it should be a high scoring game. You can give me a critique on my performance next Monday."

Both laughed at the prospect as Eddie started for the door.

Excitement in Athens was rampant, unmatched since 1980, the year the Bulldogs won the National Championship. Fans who couldn't travel to Jacksonville for the annual Georgia/Florida game finished necessary tasks early to get ready for the evening game. The streets would be almost empty by kick-off, with fans seated in front of a television, either at home or in a sports bar.

Eddie was on his second trip to the neighborhood convenience store to get more chips, salsa and cokes. The first batch of supplies was consumed by his parents and their friends during the sports shows giving the preliminaries and build-up for the game.

Eddie glanced over his right shoulder, noting the beige Ford sedan was still present. The car had followed him since he left his house. He increased his pace, cut across the street to the opposite sidewalk and slowed to a stroll. The car slowed as well. He jogged back to his original direction, darting into a narrow alley. Without looking back, he ran through the trash-littered alley and out onto the adjacent street.

The shadowing car rounded the corner and took up position about thirty feet behind him. Tiring of the game, Eddie stepped to the edge of the sidewalk and waved the car forward.

Billings lowered the darkened window on the passenger side and leaned out. "Eddie, thanks for stopping for a chat."

Eddie didn't appreciate the humor and jammed his hands in the front pockets of his jeans. With a sullen look, he stared down the street, refusing to make eye contact with Billings.

Anderson switched off the ignition. He cursed under his breath at the much abused engine as it knocked a few times before it died. Opening his door, he stepped onto the pavement, motioning for his partner to remain in the car.

Eddie stepped away, uncomfortable with the prospect of being between the two detectives. His discomfort lessened when he heard Billings whisper his assurance they were not there to arrest him.

Anderson removed a toothpick from between his teeth, flipping it into the street. "How are you doing, Eddie?"

"I'm doing okay."

"Good. Glad to hear it. We need to clarify something you told us on the night your friend died. We won't keep you long. I'm sure you want to watch the big game on television. We'll have to find it on radio while we patrol the streets."

Eddie chewed his lower lip and scuffed his ratty sneakers on the curb.

"What do you need to know?"

Anderson opened the back door and waved Eddie in.

Eddie backed away, his hands up in front of him as if to fend off Anderson. "He said you weren't going to arrest me." He pointed at Billings.

"Nobody is arresting you and we aren't going anywhere. I'm dead tired and I need to sit down."

Eddie looked hesitant but he crawled into the car, as there was little choice. Once he was seated, the door closed and he recalled that police cars did not have handles on the inside of the back doors. Sweat popped out on his forehead.

Anderson returned to his seat, letting out a big sigh as he settled in and closed the door. He listened to Billings quizzing Eddie, who apparently was more comfortable with Billings. He didn't interrupt.

"Eddie, you told us at the station the night your friend died, that Timmy got drugs from a Hispanic, named Carlos. That your best recollection?"

Eddie swallowed hard. "Yes."

"Had you ever been with Timmy when he made purchases from anyone else, other than Carlos?"

Eddie squirmed in the seat. Due to his earlier cooperation, they had not charged him with anything, not even possession, but that could change.

"Just answer the questions, Eddie. Nothing you tell us will be recorded. We are not interested in prosecuting you or the girls. We are after the people higher up."

"I've never bought any of the drugs myself, because I never had the money," Eddie said slowly. "I was with Timmy many times when he made buys. Usually we bought from Carlos or Rafael, but I remember one time we made a purchase from a guy named Pete. I think he's married to Carlos' sister."

Billings nodded, encouraging him to continue. "Were you with Timmy when he bought the drugs he used at the lake?"

"No. Timmy had to make an appearance at Sanford Stadium for his brother's ball game or his father would have given him hell. He made sure his father saw him and then he slipped out of the stadium. He met

Carlos and bought the drugs before he picked me up. On the way to the lake, we picked up the girls at Maria's house. We listened to the game on radio while driving to Lake Oconee."

Anderson interjected, "Had Timmy ever bought cocaine before?"

"No. We never did hard drugs, just pot, Ecstasy and some Quaaludes. Timmy told us he had something special when we first got in the Jeep. He didn't mention it on the way to the lake and I forgot about it. I don't believe Carlos would do anything to hurt Timmy," Eddie said. "He liked us and we liked him. I mean, it was more than just a dealer thing. We weren't close friends or anything like that, but we never put him down and Timmy was always buying him shirts, cowboy hats and things like that."

Billings gave a nod to Anderson and turned back to Eddie. "Can we drop you off somewhere?"

"No. I mean I have to go to the store, but I can walk. Are you through with me?"

Anderson reached over the seat and grasped his shoulder gently. "We're through. You have helped us a lot."

Billings got out of the car and opened the back door. He gave Eddie a pat on the back, and watched him walk away before he returned to his seat. "Well, partner. What do you think?"

Anderson leaned forward, switched on the ignition and pulled away from the curb. "I think we need to find Carlos. I believe the kid. This doesn't sound like something Carlos would do. If he didn't, who did and why?"

CHAPTER 27

After thirty-six hours of torrential rain dumped on the Florida coast courtesy of Tropical Storm Suzanne, the football field at Alltel Stadium in Jacksonville was a quagmire. The weather pattern was unusual for late fall but the planners for the annual gathering didn't worry about the weather keeping the faithful away. By game time the stands were full in spite of the downpour that soaked players and fans alike. The winner of this game would have an inside track on advancement to the Southeastern Conference Championship game.

The white chalk lines on the field were almost obliterated, causing much concern to the officials who attempted to place the ball at the appropriate spot after each play. The game was somewhat comical to those with little at stake. The players sloshed through the mud and ankle-deep water on their pass patterns and, often as not, when they caught the ball they were unable to maintain their footing and slid along the ground with the defensive player astride them.

The hard-core fans who remained in the stands throughout the game were rewarded with an epic defensive struggle, with neither team enjoying an advantage from the wretched elements. The players, while miserable from the conditions, did not let it dampen their spirits and both teams gave maximum effort.

Joshua trotted to the sideline during a timeout taken by Georgia. He grabbed the towel offered by one of the equipment guys, wiping water and mud from his face. Throwing the ball was almost impossible. Thus the game was being decided in the trenches with the offensive line doing their best to open a small hole for the Bulldogs' ball carriers. Their present offensive drive had moved the ball from Georgia's own twenty-two-yard line to Florida's twelve, taking seven minutes off the game clock.

Georgia needed to score a touchdown. Kicking a field goal would be difficult and would leave them one point down with only two minutes remaining in the game. That situation would be too precarious.

The quarterback coach stood at Joshua's side, listening to the offensive coordinator explain the next series of plays. Nodding his approval, the coach turned back to the sideline as Joshua pulled on his helmet and trotted toward the offensive huddle.

Joshua had a huge lump in his throat. This was the moment of truth. He had control. Make sure the next two plays failed and the decision to kick the field goal would be on the coach. He looked into the faces focused on him in the huddle. Trusting faces. Teammates who had struggled hard and counted on him to get the win and continue their perfect season.

He relayed the plays suggested by the offensive coordinator and clapped his hands, sending the team to the line of scrimmage.

Pete finished the last of his Budweiser, tossing the empty toward the trash can beside the refrigerator. The aluminum can bounded off the side of the cabinet and rattled across the floor clanging against the other cans from previous misses. He turned toward Carlos, who sat on the sofa observing Pete roar his approval of Georgia's win.

"That was a fucking great game, Carlos. The Dogs beat the Gators and carried the line. My bookie is going to be pissed. I loaded up on this game and that asshole thought he had a sure winner. He swore there was no way Georgia could beat Florida, much less by three points. I hope the fucking redneck kept all the action himself and didn't lay off any of it."

Carlos bowed his head, thanking God for the win, but for a different reason. Maybe Pete's jovial mood would cause him to lighten up. He had been on Carlos' ass since he walked in the door because he had not called while he was gone. Things had quieted down with the Smith investigation but in the past two weeks, since his return, there had been two more murders, which had stunned Pete.

The vinyl-covered sofa, patched in several places with duct tape, squeaked when Carlos leaned forward to grab some Corn Nuts from the bowl. Resting his elbows on his knees, he munched on the salty nuggets, working up his courage.

"Pete. The time down south gave me time to think about a lot of things. There is not much of a future for me here... sometime the cops will get me, either for being illegal or pushing dope. I have decided to make my way back out to Texas and slip back across the border."

Pete picked up the remote and increased the volume of the post-game show. He showed no reaction to Carlos' statement.

Carlos slumped back on the sofa, staring at him. After several seconds of continued silence, Carlos closed his eyes and listened to the drone of the sportscasters. His brief moment of daydreaming was shattered by a hard slap to his left ear. He opened his eyes to see Pete standing over him, foaming at the mouth.

"Who the fuck you think you are? You think you going to come in my house and tell me what your plans are? I make the plans around here. You ain't going nowhere, you fucking wetback, unless I tell you to."

Carlos jumped to his feet, his arms thrust in front of him to ward off any further blows. "I am not going to do what you say anymore. I need you if I stay here. I do not need you in Mexico."

A sneer spread across Pete's face. "Well, look here. We have us a brave little Mexican, and I emphasize the 'little' because unless you get your head right, I'm going to stomp the shit out of you."

Carlos was little in stature only and he used his stringy muscular legs to propel himself toward Pete, catching him off guard. Pete tried to step back to regain his balance but his feet became entangled and he fell to the floor, his fat ass bouncing a couple of times.

"You've fucked up," he roared. "Leave if you want to, but your sister is going to pay the price. I'll mess her up once a week, just as payback."

Carlos pounced on him like an alley cat in a territorial fight. He clawed at Pete's face and locked his wiry hands around Pete's obese neck, squeezing with all his might.

Pete's face turned blue, his eyes bulging, as he gasped for air. He pulled at Carlos' arms, trying to break the grip but the little Mexican's strength was infused by fury. Pete began to feel lightheaded from the lack of oxygen and was on the verge of blacking out when he heard a loud thump and felt Carlos' hands fall away.

Belita screamed at Carlos. "What are you doing? You are about to kill Pete."

Carlos rolled away from Pete and stared at his sister, who was brandishing a heavy metal pot. "I was trying to kill him and if he ever hits you again, I will come back and finish the job."

Belita dropped the pan and knelt at Carlos' side. "What do you mean, come back? Where are you going this time?"

Carlos got to his feet, his eyes locked on Pete. "I go back to Mexico. Pete set me up for something I did not do and the cops are going to catch up with me. They will deport me to rot in some stinking jail. I am not doing so good here anyway. I can be poor back at home without someone after me all the time."

Belita wrapped her arms around Carlos, placing herself between him and Pete. "Please don't leave. You are the only family I have."

Pete started to rise but stopped his movement when he saw Carlos push Belita aside.

Carlos stepped away from both of them and without another word, walked from the house.

CHAPTER 28

Though the surroundings were unchanged from his previous visit, Joshua was uncomfortable, lines of stress across his forehead. In spite of his objections to the location, Manuel had insisted they meet here.

He was in contact with Carlos on a daily basis and learned from him that Manuel refused to meet anyone for drug purchases; instead, his underlings were sent to make the deals. When he told Carlos about the meeting, Carlos was surprised Manuel would come out of his self-imposed exile.

Joshua had kept the information of the football scam to himself. No one else knew except Manuel, who was likely rabid over the Georgia win. Joshua patted his jacket pocket to assure the presence of the Glock. The confrontation with Manuel might become violent.

The wait was shorter than the previous time. The guttural roar from the motorcycle echoed across the desolate area, announcing Manuel's arrival.

Joshua tensed when Manuel leaped from the bike as soon as it stopped rolling.

"Goddamn you, kid. You totally fucked me. I lost my entire load on that game. Now I got nothing to work with. My business has gone to hell. People keep ending up dead."

He searched Joshua's face for any changes in his expression. "You do know that the guy I sent to make the deal with you was killed sitting is his car? It doesn't make sense. My informant in the police department told me a couple of packets of cocaine were found in the trunk and two thousand in cash was in a foil wrapper in his jacket. So it happened after you were there, but it wasn't a robbery. You wouldn't know what happened out there, would you?"

Joshua ignored Manuel's question. "I'm not eager to be caught or become a target. What's so urgent we have to meet out here again?"

The veins in Manuel's neck bulged; his stare was cold blooded. "I've got to score a big hit or I'm finished. Only thing I got left is money that belongs to the MAN. I can't lose it or I'm as good as dead."

"Who's the MAN?" Joshua questioned, his guts in a knot.

Manuel's lip curled into a sinister sneer. "You make sure Georgia loses to Auburn and I'll tell you."

Joshua's facial expression didn't change; his voice was calm. "No."

Manuel pivoted as he pushed off the Jeep's bumper and smashed into Joshua's midsection, hurling him to the ground. His big hands encircled Joshua's neck, squeezing so hard, the skin on his hands blanched white.

Joshua tried to pull Manuel's hands from his neck. His own hands searched for Manuel's face, jamming his thumbs into the orbits, in an attempt to gouge out his eyes.

Manuel, screaming in pain, released his hold on Joshua's neck and grabbed his arms.

The two men rolled across the ground, knocking the motorcycle off its stand. Joshua's face was pressed against the foot rest. He fought back when Manuel attempted to shove his head under the bike.

"I'll teach you a lesson, you smart-ass kid," Manuel screamed.

The familiarity of street fighting was to Manuel's advantage but Joshua was blessed with youth, agility and athleticism. He swung both legs up to gain leverage, and managed to hook one leg around Manuel's head. He brought his other leg up, interlocked his feet and with all his strength, jerked both legs down, breaking Manuel's hold and sending him tumbling across the ground.

By the time Joshua extricated himself from under the motorcycle, he saw Manuel on his feet pointing a Beretta at him. He held both hands in front of his face. "Shoot me, and you got no one to work your scam for you."

"You think you got me, kid. You don't know me well enough. Right now I'd rather have the pleasure of watching you beg for your life, than make all the money in the world. Get on your knees, you bastard."

Joshua brought his knees under him, calculating the distance to Manuel. If he went for Manuel's legs, he might throw him down and even if he got off a shot, it might miss or not hit a vital area. There was no possibility of getting to his own weapon.

Manuel backed up while keeping the automatic centered on Joshua's forehead. "Let's hear it. Tell me why you want to live. For mommy, and that hot little bitch you sport around. Tell me the team needs you. You can be sure I'll remind you that I gave you a choice, and you blew it. Now start begging, you playboy prick, or I'll start with your knees and work up to your eyes."

Tension hung in the air as Joshua awaited the shot from Manuel's gun; instead, he heard a sound like a watermelon bursting on pavement. He opened his eyes and saw Manuel pitch backwards, his arms flailing in the air. A micro-second later, a loud crack came from the trees.

Joshua stayed on the ground, his eyes searching the trees around him. He saw no one. He remained in the prone position for several minutes before he moved toward the Jeep. Passing Manuel's body, he saw the large mush of brain and blood lying on the ground. The back of the head was gone, in contrast to the small entrance wound in the left center of his forehead.

The Jeep seemed miles away, but he got to the driver's door and swung it open. Crawling into the seat, he anticipated the shot that would end his life as well, but it never came. He drove with reckless speed from the area, his mind racing with thoughts, all of them unwanted and undesirable.

CHAPTER 29

Anderson approached Bill Stewart, who was sitting in a chair partially blocking the entrance to the Chief of Detectives' office. The portly man's face glowed redder than usual when Anderson, without acknowledgement, walked past him and plopped down in the chief's chair. Anderson knew Assistant Chief Stewart hated him so he never let an opportunity pass by if it would in anyway get the AC riled up.

"Anderson, get your ass out of the chief's chair!"

In response, Anderson put his feet up on the desk, leaning back in the large high-backed chair. The smile on his face spread even wider. "Fuck you, AC."

"What did you say?" Stewart screamed.

Anderson stared at the ceiling, shaking his head. "Damn, Stewart. Not only are you a total dickhead, but you're also fucking deaf."

Stewart's reply was interrupted by the entrance of Chief McElroy, who appeared in no mood to referee a pissing contest between his subordinates. Following close behind the chief through the door was Roxanne, his receptionist and girl Friday. As usual, she was dressed to kill, in a short skirt and a silk blouse with ample cleavage exposed, highlighting the assets that got her the job.

Chief McElroy wasted little time in sorting things out. "Anderson, wait in the outer office but don't leave. I've got to talk to you after I'm finished with Stewart. Roxanne, get me some coffee."

Anderson sat on the edge of Roxanne's desk, biding his time by spinning the dial on the Rolodex. He smiled at Roxanne when she passed by with the coffee for the chief.

Less than a minute later, she returned and motioned for Anderson to enter the chief's office. Opening the door, he almost collided with Stewart, who was making a hasty exit. The color of his face had not improved.

Chief McElroy was facing the window with the back of the chair toward Anderson. He remained silent for a few moments before he turned the chair to face Anderson, who stood near the edge of the large desk.

"Have a seat, Doug." The chief motioned for Anderson to sit on the leather sofa to the right of the desk. "What do you think of the Bulldogs? Think they're good enough to compete for the national championship this year?"

Anderson was caught off guard by the informality and by a question so unrelated to the reason he was at the office. He sat slack-jawed, feeling like the village idiot while he squirmed on the sofa. He stammered out his response. "Uh, I haven't kept up with them that well. I know they got a hot-shot quarterback, a local boy, I believe, but I don't catch all of the games. What are they now—seven wins, no losses?"

McElroy smiled at Anderson. "Don't try to bullshit me, Doug. You know that local boy is Joshua Smith. His dad is a prominent physician in our fair city and a big contributor to our auxiliary. You got the record right. Pardon my lame attempt at small talk but I didn't think it proper to start chewing your ass without saying hello," the chief said.

"Now that we've got the civilities out of the way, let me ask you a question. Just what in the hell are you and Billings doing? The mayor just verbally lopped off a large piece of my ass about the time and money this department is spending on this investigation. Along with some other prominent Athenians, he's concerned about your harassment of Joshua Smith. More important to me, why haven't you produced something to show for all the resources you've spent?"

Anderson let the chief rave, well aware that McElroy was his biggest supporter and just needed to vent his frustration. He didn't like interference from the politicians anymore than Anderson, but he was closer to the top and absorbed much of the crap that flowed downhill. The chief understood that sometimes there was nothing to show for the expenditure of time and manpower, no matter the effort made. This fact was often lost on the administration.

Anderson started to speak but was interrupted by a steady buzz from the phone on the desk.

McElroy picked up the hand set, pressed the blinking light on the base and motioned for Anderson to remain seated. He waited a couple of seconds before speaking. "Chief McElroy."

Anderson turned his attention away from the chief. He looked back over his shoulder when the door opened and saw Billings making a pointed gesture at his watch. Anderson shrugged his shoulders in resignation, returning his attention to the chief, now sitting with his back to Anderson.

In his years of police work, Anderson had learned that politicians made the Chief of Detectives' job a living hell. The chief was expected to assure the safety of the citizens of the community and he had to do it with limited manpower and financial resources. Equally frustrating, he had the added weight of making sure that certain friends of his political bosses were not offended or inconvenienced. This was one of those occasions. Anderson noticed the back of the chief's neck turn red, then the redness spread up to his ears. The conversation was one-sided, the chief listening with no response other than periodic grunts.

The pencil in the chief's hand snapped. He tossed the broken pieces into a wastebasket at the corner of his desk. He leaned forward in his chair, his arms resting on his knees.

Anderson remained silent. It was apparent the chief was being dressed down by someone and Anderson felt sure the wrath would soon descend on him, when the phone conversation was over.

After an eternity of three or so minutes, McElroy replaced the phone on the cradle. He remained in the same position with his back to Anderson, his attention focused out the window. A pigeon landed on the window sill but didn't appear to interrupt the chief's thoughts.

Without turning around, he finally spoke. "Anderson, you and Billings are costing this department a lot of money and manpower just to find out who's capping those drug dealers. Nobody gives a shit about them being wasted and that's not for public consumption. Still, it's the truth, and the chairman of the Board of Commissioners just gave me a refresher course in exactly those words."

McElroy's gruff voice rumbled on. "Personally, I don't give a damn if every drug dealer in north Georgia is killed, if our own good citizens aren't involved. It would make life easier for all of us. We'll have another little talk soon, but for now get back to your other duties and let this thing drop."

Anderson stared at the back of the chief's chair. Getting up from the sofa, he responded, "Yes, sir." As he pulled the door to the office closed, he saw the chief was still staring out the window.

Billings looked up from a magazine when Anderson stopped beside him. "Well, partner. What's our next move?"

Anderson felt as if he would vomit. "You knew he was going to pull us off the cases, didn't you?"

Billings shook his head with resignation. He stood, gripping Anderson by the shoulder. "Not really, partner, not this very day, but everyone around here suspected it would happen sooner or later. It seems you are the only one who cares if the perps are caught or not."

Anderson's temper flared. He kicked a chair, sending it across the wooden floor slamming into the wall adjacent to Roxanne's desk. She clutched her large bosom in surprise. Anderson railed out at Billings.

"What the hell is wrong with you people? Murder is murder. It shouldn't matter if the victim is a dirt bag or a saint."

Billings retrieved the chair, sliding it back to its normal place. "Doug, listen to me. Do you think for a minute 'Joe Citizen' gives a damn if we find out who's killing the scum of the street? Hell, the public is happy the bad guys are doing each other. It's like the gang-bangers out in California and in New York. Who cares if they have wars and kill each other? The police get involved when the innocent get hurt. Man, get a grip on yourself. You've got this obsession to solve every case and it's driving you nuts. Hell, you're driving us all nuts."

Anderson glared at his partner before he noticed Roxanne cringing in her chair with a look of disbelief. He murmured an apology and left the office.

Billings picked up his coat, turning to Roxanne. "He'll be okay. I'll burn him a steak at my house tonight. My wife and I will get him drunk."

CHAPTER 30

Anderson glanced at his rear view mirror. The small pickup truck was still there. He had picked up on the tail soon after he left his office and purposely drove home at a leisurely speed so not to lose his tracker. He toyed with the idea of calling a black-and-white to drop in behind the truck but changed his mind. He didn't want to scare off whoever was back there.

He turned into his driveway, noting his tail followed him, parking just off the street. Anderson switched off the ignition, exited his SUV and walked back to the truck. He kept his hand on the weapon in his shoulder holster. When he recognized Carlos in the driver's seat, Anderson dropped his hand and opened the door of the truck.

Anderson sat at the kitchen table in his apartment. He took a swallow of beer, watching the slightly built Hispanic, known to him as Carlos, squirm in the chair across the table. Anderson stared at him, willing Carlos to make eye contact. Instead the little Mexican constantly shifted in the chair, his discomfort obvious.

Anderson waited a few more seconds, allowing Carlos to feel the heat before he spoke. "I have stayed off your back. You told us you would cooperate but you haven't told us shit. Now it's payback time. If you feed me a bunch of bullshit, I'll find you and make your life miserable."

Carlos looked at Anderson, his glassy eyes reflecting his fear. "I do not lie to you. I will help if you not send me back to Mexico."

Anderson nodded. "I can't state one hundred percent that you won't get sent back but it will go in your favor if you help us catch the people who are killing the dealers. Plus we need information so we can bust up the whole drug operation. Now, what can you tell me? And it better be good."

"I no longer live with Pete and my sister. We fight and I tell them I go back to Mexico but I not want to."

Anderson nodded. "Why did you fight?"

"Pete is getting crazy scared. Dealers are getting killed. He doesn't want to leave the house. He try to make me do everything. I tell him no. He threatened to hurt my sister and I choke him. My sister hit me—*me*, to stop me. She protect Pete rather than me."

"So you went after Pete?" Anderson laughed at his mental vision of the episode. "What else has made Pete so scared?"

Carlos glanced around the room, afraid someone was present who might overhear his conversation. He wiped the sweat from his face. "There is new guy in town. They call him Danny Weber. He is short, but taller than me. He built like a truck and mean. He take Manuel's place, but he no Mexican. White guy with short hair and tattoos all over. Everybody scared of him. Always three amigos with him, everywhere he goes."

Anderson leaned closer. "Have you met him? Made any deals?"

"No... no. No deal with him. I am small fish, but I see him with others. He tell everyone, he kill anybody that fuck with him."

"Where's he hanging out?"

Carlos hesitated and then shook his head. "He goes all over but I hear talk about a place, called Arcade."

Sweat dripped from Anderson's brow. The evening air was cool but the small duplex apartment was poorly ventilated and held heat like an oven. He wiped the sweat with his shirt sleeve. "Who do you know that has been there?"

Carlos got up from his chair with an abrupt movement and stood near the wall by the refrigerator, his eyes darting in the direction of the back door.

"Don't even think about running, Carlos. That door is locked with a keyed dead bolt and you ain't getting the key."

Carlos covered his face with his hands. "If I tell, he will kill me."

"No one will know. If you keep your mouth shut about what we discuss, you'll be okay."

A sly grin spread across Anderson's face, and his eyes narrowed. "If you don't tell me, I'll drive you down to the south side, put your skinny ass on the street, and let the word out you fingered Weber."

Carlos made his way back to the chair, his legs suddenly weak. It took less than fifteen seconds for him to make his decision. "Pete. You know him, I think. He marries my sister two years ago. She sent me money to come here. I got work cutting grass and cleaning yards. Made good money, but Pete laughed at me. Said it would take me forever to make enough money to get help to be legal. He told me he had a quicker way. He made me work for him. Said he will turn me in, if I do not."

Carlos licked his lips, swallowing hard, his throat dry. "He takes me around town. Show me places boys and girls hang ... uh ... together."

"You mean hangouts?"

"That's right, hangouts," Carlos said.

Anderson got up and retrieved a couple of beers from the refrigerator. He handed a cold Michelob to Carlos and returned to his chair. "So, what was your job? What do you do for Pete?"

Carlos drained the bottle before he lowered it. "I make friends with the boys, sometimes the girls. I sell them very small bags of grass and some tablets. I sell cheap."

"Marijuana, okay. What kind of tablets?"

Carlos placed the empty bottle on the table. He licked his lips, eying the refrigerator.

"Go ahead," answered Anderson to the silent question.

Carlos took more time with the second bottle, and seemed more relaxed now. "They buy all kind of pills—speed, Valium, Ecstasy. Sometimes buy one tablet, sometimes two or three."

Anderson leaned forward, puzzled. "Why such small amounts?"

"Not much money. They buy only little bit."

"These weren't college kids, were they?"

Carlos shook his head. "Not little kids, but old enough to drive cars."

"High school," Anderson said.

Carlos nodded.

"Do you ever pick up a large amount of anything for Pete?"

"No. Pete always do that. He only gives me little bit. I give money back to him. He gives me some to spend, but he keeps most. He say he keep it for me for later. But I not believe him."

"Were you ever with Pete when he got the bigger supply?"

"I went sometimes, but after Manuel got killed, Pete not take me anymore. Said the new man not want many people around."

"Does Pete meet with Weber often?"

Carlos ran his hand through his oily hair. "Not sure. I know Pete has new supply each week. He keeps at his house and gives out to me and some others, but I only one that gets it from his house. He takes it to the others at their special meeting places."

Anderson picked up his bottle, turning it in his hand. "Does Pete know Weber's supplier?"

Carlos was on his feet again, pacing back and forth in the small kitchen. "I don't know. I don't think so."

With a wave of his hand, Anderson indicated for Carlos to sit back down. "Why are you so nervous when we talk about Weber? Has Pete told you something?"

The little Mexican held onto the back of the chair, but did not sit. "Pete says it not good to know too much."

Knowledge gained by years of interrogation told Anderson he was getting close to a sensitive area. "There's a bigger man in Athens, someone much bigger than Weber."

Carlos began shaking, the chair banging against the table. He stared at Anderson, fear evident in his eyes, but he did not answer. Finally he sat down again. "There's a truck delivery coming. Pete talks about this truck and it always comes just before we have a lot more to sell. I heard Pete talk to Weber on the phone about the delivery time. He not say exactly where, but I think I know, from what I heard Pete say."

"Just relax, Carlos. You're doing great. Let me get a map out of my desk and you show me where you think it will be delivered."

Carlos looked drained but managed a smile. "What about my sister?"

"Don't worry. You come through on this, and it will go a long way toward helping you and your sister."

Anderson felt hopeful for the first time in weeks. If they could score a hit with a good raid, they might get to Weber. He was the link to the MAN.

Nothing smoothed the ruffled feathers of the Drug Task Force quicker than action. Realizing he was losing the cohesiveness of his team, Chief McElroy agreed to the raid after reviewing the new intelligence from Anderson. The data was sketchy at best and, false at worst but it was time to take action.

"Anderson, don't crap out on this. I've used up all my favors downtown. If you have any doubts about this mission, let me hear it. We can postpone this until we get more solid leads."

Anderson fidgeted in his chair, his emotions waging a battle between his loyalty to the chief and his need to get something done. He was out on a limb with this but he couldn't back down. "It's as good as anything we've had lately."

"Jesus Christ, Anderson. That's not what I need to hear. I want you to tell me it is rock solid, a sure thing, something that's going to get the commissioners off my ass."

The chief pushed back from his desk, rising with caution from the chair, his back impaired from bullet wounds sustained in the line of duty years earlier. Anderson knew that McElroy's years of experience helped him understand what the detectives faced every day: thus the chief's willingness to fight the politicians for them.

Anderson remained silent, giving the chief time to rationalize his decision. He anticipated he would get the go-ahead, even if the chief had to put his own career on the line.

The big man walked around the desk and stood in front of Anderson. "Take Team Alpha and Team Bravo, and take one unit from SWAT. You don't know what kind of firepower you'll be facing, so be on the cautious side. Try not to make it a neighborhood war. I've got enough heat on me from the media already."

Anderson noted the smile on the chief's face. He grasped the extended hand, accepting the handshake "to go with the chief's blessing." Knowing when it was time to cut and run, he retreated from the room before the chief changed his mind.

Saturday nights in a college town, especially during football season, were wild and rambunctious. Most of the citizens wisely kept their families at home watching television and enjoying home delivery pizza. This particular Saturday night in Athens, after the Bulldogs defeated the Auburn Tigers, was anything but usual, and wild did not adequately define the goings-on in the downtown area.

The ratio of drunk students to sober individuals defied the imagination, and parents back home in small town, USA, did not want to see their intelligent, law-abiding youngsters staggering half-naked on video during the eleven o'clock news. So, most didn't watch.

In a different section of town, things were much quieter. A warehouse located on the Winder highway, just inside the Athens city limits, was the immediate focus of Anderson, Billings, and the SWAT team hidden around the building. The SWAT team members had been dropped off hours earlier; the assault vehicles parked several miles away. They remained in constant radio contact with Anderson and Billings who were in an unmarked car, parked at an abandoned service station. They all had been in position for almost four hours and were getting antsy about the lack of activity.

Billings checked his shoulder holster again, reassuring himself that his weapon was in place. It was at least the tenth time he had checked it in the last five minutes. It didn't bother him. It did bother Anderson, who was about to explode from anticipation.

"Damn that Carlos. If he sent us on a wild goose chase, I'll string his scrawny ass up on a pole and beat him like a piñata."

Billing chuckled. "Take it easy. He said the delivery was expected tonight. He didn't say what time."

Anderson reached behind the front seat to retrieve the thermos of coffee. The fullness in his bladder made him change his mind. "Damn, partner. I've got to take a whiz again. I'm glad you thought to remove the lamp from the overhead light."

"I had to learn something from all these years on stakeout with you. You need to see a doctor about that little bladder of yours."

"My bladder's fine. It's just all the rot-gut coffee we drink sitting out here all damn night. What are you, a damn camel? You haven't been since we got here."

"Just a matter of mental toughness, my friend. You know, mind over matter."

"Bullshit," replied Anderson, climbing out of the car. He was in the midst of his relief when he saw headlights flash across the front of the warehouse.

The dingy white of the painted concrete structure reflected the lights of a large truck approaching the building. It stopped in front of the large hangar-type doors and someone jumped out from the passenger side of the truck. Using the light from the truck, the individual located a side door to the building, fumbled with a set of keys, and entered. Several moments later, the large doors swung open and the truck drove inside.

Anderson finished his business squatting alongside the car. He grimaced when he felt the wetness of the front of his pants. When he opened the door, he heard Billings on the radio, already in contact with the SWAT team.

"Cover all the doors and windows. Team Alpha—take up position on each side of the hangar doors. SWAT team—be prepared to breach the side door if it's locked. Team Bravo, post yourselves at the rear of the building."

Anderson looked around the area, searching for any vehicles that might have inadvertently driven into the scene. He gave the all clear signal to Billings.

"Go. Go. Go," Billings shouted into the handset.

Anderson roared out of their hiding place, racing across the highway into the warehouse lot. Before they were out of the car, the SWAT team had breached the closed doors of the building and had the two occupants surrounded. Their action was so quick, the two men inside had no choice except immediate surrender.

Billings, followed by Anderson, charged through the hangar doors opened by Team Alpha. The two men from the truck were lying on their sides, bound by plastic ties on their feet and wrists.

Anderson called to the SWAT team leader, "Have your explosives expert check the truck for booby traps. We need to get in the back of the truck as fast as we can."

Several members of the team swarmed over the truck like ants. Within minutes the team leader reported to Anderson. "It's clear, sir."

"Break the lock on the back doors and swing them open. Get a ladder or something over here so we can move things out of the truck."

A moment later, one of the men spoke. "No need, sir. There's a built-in ramp. When we slide it out, we can easily unload the truck." The man reached for the lever for the ramp release.

"Wait," shouted Anderson. "Check the railing on the ramp. Make sure it's not wired to explosives somewhere inside the truck."

The SWAT team leader slid under the truck and inspected the rails on both sides of the ramp. "It's clear, sir, but good thinking."

Once the ramp was released and extended from the truck, Billings and Anderson moved into the interior and found several large wooden crates. All the team members worked together to lift the crates out of the truck and lined them up against a far wall.

Billings turned to the team leader. "Have a couple of your men sweep the interior of the truck for trap doors or hidden compartments. We'll get into the crates and see what Santa has brought us for an early Christmas."

Someone produced a crowbar, and began opening the crates.

Billings separated loose straw in the first crate, extracted a masonry figure of an angel and threw it to the cement floor. The figurine shattered and pieces scattered about the floor. There was nothing inside. They repeated the procedure with the contents of three of the large crates. All they had to show for their efforts was a large pile of broken masonry. The men stared at the pile with looks of frustration.

Anderson kicked at the pile, sending broken pieces sailing like miniature soccer balls. He turned toward the SWAT team leader. "What did you learn from the two occupants?"

"Nothing, sir. They said they were paid to drive this truck from Laredo, Texas, to this building. That's all they know."

"A rat's ass," Billings responded. "Contract drivers aren't given the key to the warehouse just to drive the truck here. Question them again. See if they have a map of the area. If they don't have a map, they know the area well and have done this before."

Anderson climbed up into the truck body and helped manhandle another crate toward the back of the truck. They were in the process of prying off the lid, when someone hollered from beneath the truck.

"Detectives, you need to see this."

Billings and Anderson crawled under the truck where Paul Wilson of Team Bravo was sprawled out on his back, his flashlight aimed upwards.

"This truck must be built for very long hauls," Wilson said. "It's got two extra fuel tanks that look to hold about seventy-five gallons each."

"Find the caps to those tanks," Anderson said.

Wilson crawled out from under the truck, following the feeder tube from the portal on the right side of the truck. He removed the cap and sniffed. "Sure smells like diesel fuel in there."

Anderson's shoulders slumped, his brief elation squashed.

Billings suddenly became animated, waving his arms. "Find me a long piece of flexible cable or plastic."

Within two minutes, Wilson returned to the truck with a six-foot length of heavy electrical wire.

Billings introduced it into the fuel portal and the wire stopped after two feet. After three more attempts, he turned to the others with a big grin on his face. "These are false tanks—just enough fuel in the feeder line to fool a quick inspection. Let's take the truck to the barn and let our guys take it apart."

He looked at Wilson. "Where did you find this wire so quickly?"

Wilson smiled. "I hope nobody tries to turn on the heat pump anytime soon."

CHAPTER 31

Silence enveloped James Smith after he finished dictation on his last patient. The stack of completed patient charts on his desk attested to his hectic day, which had drained him mentally and physically.

He glanced again at the newspaper he had previously thrown to the floor. The headlines written in bold letters across the front page proclaimed a recent drug raid a huge success. Accompanying the story was a picture of the truck that had been disassembled, revealing the stash of illicit drugs in the false fuel tanks.

The paper was only a reminder of the event. He had actually been a witness. From a hiding place in a paint store across from the warehouse, he had watched the truck arrive. He personally never attended the transfer of a shipment. Instead he left the task to Weber and his hand-picked men. He made it a point to watch unseen the arrival of each shipment, so Weber couldn't rip off the drugs by claiming they didn't arrive.

The SWAT team had been too eager to intercept the shipment and missed the chance of snagging Weber and his people, who had been delayed by engine trouble. Had Weber been there, it would not have gone down so peacefully, Smith knew. The man was a crazy bastard and would have shot his way out of the trap rather than be captured.

Smith had remained in the paint shop, which he owned through a false corporation, for several hours before sneaking out the back. He had parked in a residential area a half mile behind the shop, safely out of sight of the police. When he arrived home, he had gone straight to his study where he remained the entire night. He had heard Joshua when he entered the house, but ignored his knocks on the study door.

The day's patient schedule had been brutal, allowing him little time to brood over the loss of the drugs and the expected wrath of Ortega. He placed the microphone on top of the charts, turned off the machine and buried his face in his hands. For the first time since his involvement in drug trafficking, he experienced fear.

The ring of the cellular phone jarred him from his moment of despair, and he fumbled with the small holster on his belt. Flipping open the phone, he stared at the caller ID listed as unknown number.

There was no problem, however, identifying the voice of Ortega, nor assessing his mood.

"What the hell is going on, Smith? You told me things were under control. Be here tomorrow night. You know where. Make it at eight."

The connection was broken before Smith had a chance to say a word. He thought it unwise of Ortega to rattle off like he did without knowing who had answered. "Damn, I'm losing it," he said out loud.

He wiped his sweaty palms on his lab coat, and then walked across the room to a wet bar hidden behind a cabinet door in the bookcase. He poured himself a shot glass of Maker's Mark, downing the smooth liquor neat in one gulp. Taking the bottle and the glass with him, he returned to his chair, where he poured another shot. Leaning back, he sipped from the small glass, waiting for the magic elixir to relieve his pounding headache.

While he rested, he tried to piece together what he would say to Ortega. His life was going to hell, and had been since Timmy died. He felt no remorse over his son's death or the fact that his wife was nearing insanity, but he felt awash with self-pity over the latest events and the destruction of his dreams. Who was doing this to him?

The party-like atmosphere in the detectives' office was a vast difference from previous days when the place resembled a morgue. Anderson and Billings enjoyed the glad tidings from their peers but recognized a lot of work remained. The chief was pacified after the news release of their success.

Photos of the stacks of cellophane-wrapped white and brown powder, along with hundreds of bottles of pills, taken from the false fuel tanks, had been prominently displayed on the front pages of the Athens and Atlanta newspapers. There were no pictures of the victorious team members, nor did they desire any. They preferred their anonymity.

With their coffee cups refilled, Anderson and Billings returned to their desks. They had already talked about the events of the raid and the disappointment both felt that no key dealers were nabbed.

"What do you think, partner, did we go in too soon?"

Anderson placed his cup on the desk top. He opened a large file while he pondered Billings' question. "Hell, I don't know. Some say we did, but if we had waited longer, we might have lost the two drivers, even if they haven't been all that helpful. We needed a bust, and we got it, so I guess we have to be happy with that."

"Don't get me wrong," Billings said. "I'm not unhappy but I can promise you, someone is very unhappy. They haven't determined a street value yet, but it's got to be in the millions. That will put a serious dent in someone's bank account."

An ear-to-ear grin appeared on Anderson's face. "It will put a dent in some heads as well. I don't care how much money these dudes have, when you lose a shipment like this one, it's got to hurt and will make some people very angry, maybe even seriously hostile. I sure am glad I'm not the one who has to answer to the MAN."

"You got that right, brother."

A buzz from Anderson's phone interrupted the bull session. He punched up the intercom, listened for a few seconds, and hung up. "McElroy wants to see us."

The two men crossed the expanse of the office, acknowledging the waves from secretaries, and were met by the chief standing in the doorway of his office. His big hand was outstretched in greeting.

"Good job, men. There will be slim pickings on the streets of Athens for a while, and with the game with Georgia Tech coming up in two weeks, the bad guys need to hustle to get things back in working order. That might work to our advantage."

"How's that, Chief?"

"They will be in a hurry to get their supply back on the street and they will use shortcuts and make mistakes in doing so. If they do, we'll be in position to take advantage of it."

Anderson ran his hand over the short stubble of hair atop his head. "This mean we get more help on the case?"

Chief McElroy locked eyes with Anderson. "Don't misunderstand me. I'm not talking about those drug dealer murders. My feelings have not changed on that. I'm talking about making hits, where we interrupt their flow of drugs and capture some of their suppliers. We might get lucky and catch a big dog. For your information, we checked out that warehouse. It's owned by a rug dealer in Atlanta who closed his business in Athens several years ago. Hasn't sold it because he hoped to reopen someday. Didn't have a clue it was being used."

Anderson was unable to hide his disappointment. "So we are to lay off the murder investigations for now."

"Okay. I know how you feel about those investigations but look at the positive press we got for the hit. That's the thing the public wants to see. I will reward the good job you and Billings have done. I'll give you a little more leeway to see what you can come up with, as long as it doesn't interfere with the main task."

Billings grabbed Anderson by the arm, directing him toward the door. "We got you, Chief. We'll get up a list of the manpower we need and, our plan of action. We'll have it ready by tomorrow."

Walking back to their desks, Anderson turned to Billings. "What's up with dragging me out of the room?"

"I know you, good buddy. The chief offered you a small morsel and you were ready to push for the whole damn meal."

The day at Smith's office seemed an eternity to the doctor. He had more important things on his mind than to pamper a bunch of rich snobs who thought they were dying just because they had the flu. He was relieved when the office closed and he was able to get out. The drive to Arcade helped him unwind and gave him a few minutes to collect his thoughts.

This would be his first meeting with Weber since they both had met with Ortega. There was much to discuss. Repair work in their supply line was needed before the Bulldogs' next game.

Smith turned off the highway, following the dirt road to an area behind Weber's cabin. When he switched off the ignition he saw Weber standing on the back porch. Each time Smith saw the man, he was again stunned to silence. The man had a larger than normal head, covered by short, stiff blond hair, resting on a stump of a body, with virtually no neck. Massive arms hung from broad shoulders and tree-trunk legs supported the large torso in between. The size of the man was frightening enough but it was accentuated by his cherub-like face. The combination was evil personified.

Weber dropped off the porch, ignoring the back steps. "No trouble finding the place, I see."

Smith accepted the offered hand, watching his own hand disappear in the ham-sized extremity. "No, the directions were right on."

They entered the cabin and sat at a wooden table. Smith looked around the interior, noting the bare walls and naked floor. Not a man for creature comforts, he thought. He brought Weber up to speed on the operation, providing more details than Ortega had in regards to the loss of the dealers.

"Any chance someone is muscling in?" Weber asked.

"I don't think so. There are no competing sales, nor any new dealers on the streets. Someone is taking out our dealers and maybe the same person or persons are feeding information to the investigators. I want you to work back through my people and see if you can find the source. Take whatever measures are necessary. Just make sure my name is never brought up. I must remain anonymous in order to be successful."

Weber nodded his understanding. "I've talked with some of the workers already and I've got a meeting set up today with Pete—the guy that worked under Manuel. He might be our best lead to any problems, since Manuel was the biggest fish taken out."

Smith didn't like being categorized as one of the fish but accepted the analogy. "Just do it as quickly and discreetly as you can. We're losing millions and we need to make it up before the college crowd goes home on Christmas break."

CHAPTER 32

The Varsity in Athens was part of the college lore. Located on the corner of West Broad and Milledge Avenue, it was a favorite eating place for university students and locals. Several fraternity and sorority houses were in close proximity, adding to the popularity. Alumni returning for football games loved to take their children to the Varsity for a "walking dog and a PC"—a hot dog and chocolate milk poured over crushed ice.

Joshua bypassed the counter, canvassing the sitting area for PJ. A quick peek at his watch revealed he was twenty minutes early. He found two vacant seats, plopped down in one and threw his backpack in the other. The place was about three-quarters full and it was unlikely anyone would challenge him for the "saved" seat. A sports announcer, beaming from a television hung high on the wall, was discussing the next year's NFL draft. Any other time Joshua would have been interested, but now his mind was occupied by other events.

It was getting harder to focus on football, much less his academics. Juggling football practice with chemistry labs and maintaining a 3.5 average was tough enough, but now with the added distractions, he was falling behind on everything. That everything included quality time with PJ, and she was becoming more vocal about it each time they met, leading to more time arguing than kissing.

His saving grace was the football season. The team was undefeated and would be in the SEC Championship game as the Eastern Division Champions. Balancing football and medicine wasn't new, Joshua thought. Several former NFL players were now physicians, but how many of them had tracked drug dealers during their careers?

Something had to give and unfortunately it had been his relationship with PJ. She had tired of the mental and emotional distance that had developed between them. Soon he would no longer be able to use football as an excuse, since the team had two weeks before they played Georgia Tech, and a month before the SEC Championship game. PJ had run out of patience and was making threats of an ultimatum.

Lost in his thoughts, Joshua was unaware she was standing next to him until he felt her touch him on the shoulder.

"Good program, huh?" she said.

Joshua blushed but quickly stood to greet her. He took her books, placed them on the floor between their seats, and removed his own book bag from the seat he had saved. "Not really, I was just killing time. I got here earlier than expected and decided to wait for you before I ordered. What would you like to order?"

PJ rested her arms on the half table section, folding one hand over the other, a mannerism he had seen often when she was troubled. "I'm not very hungry. Just order me a Diet Coke, please."

Joshua returned within a few minutes with a plastic tray loaded down with hot dogs, fries, and a Diet Coke.

PJ stared at the tray and remarked in an icy tone, "Apparently nothing is wrong with your appetite."

"Excuse me, should there be?" He handed her a Diet Coke, taking the seat beside her.

She held the glass in her trembling hands, making no move to drink. "I mean, you've been acting so weird lately, I thought you might be depressed or something. You don't spend time with me, you ignore your friends, and you spend more time with Eddie than any of the rest of us. I thought he was Timmy's friend. Why have you become so taken with him?"

Joshua took a bite of his hot dog; a drop of mustard oozed out, dripping onto his chin. He dabbed at it with a napkin and continued to chew, using the moment to gather his thoughts. The more he chewed, the larger the bite seemed to grow in his mouth. He took a big gulp of his drink to wash it down. His appetite was gone and he pushed the food away.

"PJ, I haven't ignored you or my friends. As for Eddie, he's hurting just like me and, I guess we just naturally gravitated to one another." He saw the frown on PJ's face. She wasn't buying his lame excuse.

Her lower lip was trembling. "I left school early a few days ago and when I walked to the parking lot, I saw a small Hispanic guy around your car. He appeared to be waiting on you. Was that Carlos that you inquired about earlier? What are you involved in, Joshua?"

The room became quiet, or so he felt—as though everyone stopped what they were doing to listen to his and PJ's conversation. His conscience was playing tricks on his mind. It was impossible to hide things from PJ. She knew him too well; at times she seemed able to read his mind.

"I can't tell you right now," he said. "I have a lot on my mind and things I need to do. But I promise you, I still love you more than anything in the world. Please believe me."

She buried her face in her hands for a moment and then looked up again, dabbing tears away with one of the napkins. "I don't doubt your love for me and never have, but I do worry that you're getting involved in something way over your head. You promised weeks ago you would tell me. Now you are still putting me off."

PJ stood up, her hand on Joshua's shoulder, implying for him to remain seated. "Maybe it would be better if we gave each other time to think about what's important to us. I'll see you at school but please don't call me for a while."

Joshua watched her leave. He did not want to lose her, but felt compelled to continue what he was doing, regardless of the sacrifice. He ignored the food and with his heart aching, he walked out.

CHAPTER 33

Eddie leaned against a metal light pole in the K Mart parking lot waiting for Pete. He searched the large expanse of asphalt, glancing repeatedly at his watch. He began to have doubts whether or not he had understood Rafael correctly. The message from Pete instructed him to be in the lot at nine o'clock tonight.

The store was still open but only a few cars were in the lot. Eddie was concerned someone might notice him standing alone in the lot for such a long time. He'd had Calvin drop him off at eight, worried that he would miss the appointment. Joshua would be pissed that he disobeyed his instructions to stay away from Pete and Carlos, but he was tired of always being in the background and wanted to prove his worth to Joshua. He had made Calvin promise not to say a word to Joshua about the meeting. He had reluctantly involved Calvin because he needed transportation to the parking lot.

Eddie thought Joshua was overreacting, telling them to let things lie for a while. After Manuel's death, the dealers were getting tighter in their security and it was harder to set up meetings. He and Calvin were shocked when Joshua told them that Pete had not shown up for the last meeting. When Eddie questioned Rafael about it, he shook his head as if he didn't understand.

Eddie watched as another person left the store, loaded their purchases in their car and drove out of the lot. He counted the cars in the lot. Seven cars remained. If Pete didn't show within the next five minutes he would start walking toward town. If he stayed, there was a good chanced he would be picked up for loitering. His problem was resolved when a metallic gray four-door Mercedes pulled up.

A white guy with blond hair and a blond mustache motioned to him to approach the car. "Hey, sport, your name Eddie?"

"You got it. I was beginning to think you wouldn't show."

"Don't bust my balls. The meeting was scheduled for nine and my watch reads nine on the dot. You still interested?"

"Yeah," Eddie replied. "Great car. I've never been in a Mercedes before."

Pete flipped a cigarette onto the pavement, sending sparks in the wind when it struck. "Not mine but get in. We'll drive around while we talk. It will be a lot less risky than sitting out here in the parking lot."

Eddie's confidence sagged. Until this moment he had never realized the pressure Joshua had been under when he met with dealers time and time again. Now, he was uncertain what to do. It had seemed so easy when he and Calvin discussed it. Calvin was to pick him up at eleven at the same spot.

He stared at Pete's smiling face and then walked around to the passenger side of the car. Opening the door, he noticed the dome light wasn't working and thought it odd on such a new car. He fastened his seat belt. When the car started in motion he began with small talk trying to ease his nervousness.

He was unaware of the person crouched down in the seat behind him.

CHAPTER 34

PJ drove into the circular drive in front of the Smiths' Williamsburg-style home. She was a frequent visitor to the house, yet still marveled at the expanse of the six-thousand-square-foot house and three-car garage. Dr. Smith kept his Mercedes sedan and his 1956 restored Corvette convertible in two of the slots. His wife's Lincoln took the third spot. Since Timmy's death her car had remained in its assigned slot. The twin black Jeep Wranglers, Joshua's and the one Timmy had driven, were parked in a paved alcove adjacent to the garage.

PJ drove her Honda Accord to the opposite side of the driveway, pulling well off the paved surface to avoid blocking the garage entrance. The triple doors were down, obscuring the inside of the parking area. She noticed Timmy's Jeep in its usual location. Joshua's vehicle was not there.

Climbing the brick steps of the front entrance, she saw a curtain move in the window above. She was familiar enough with the layout of the house to know the window was to Timmy's bedroom, and she suspected the person separating the white material covering the window was Connie Smith.

PJ pressed the doorbell and stood back to allow whoever answered the door to see her on the stoop. A full minute passed. She reached for the button again just as the door opened. Although she had seen Connie several times since the funeral, she was still taken aback by her appearance. The woman was shriveled up, a shell of her previously beautiful body.

Connie managed a brief smile, opening the door wider for PJ to enter. "PJ, what a pleasant surprise. I didn't know you were coming or I would have made myself a little more presentable."

PJ took Connie's hands in her own, giving her a reassuring squeeze. "Nonsense, you look beautiful at any time of the day. I'm sorry if I'm interrupting your afternoon. I came by to speak to Joshua. Since the team didn't practice today, I thought he might be at home."

Connie ushered her into the foyer, closing the front door before she answered. "He must be at the library. I heard him say this morning at breakfast that he needed to get some research material he couldn't find on the internet. He's been such a dear, driving over early in the morning just to have breakfast with me. I know his schedule is much too busy to be doing that."

PJ was puzzled by the comment. She took many of the same courses as Joshua but didn't remember any papers due. Maybe it isn't related to school, she thought.

Connie took her by the arm. "Why don't you wait in James' study until Joshua gets home? You'll be more comfortable in here and you will be able to see him when he comes in the front door."

"Okay, thanks." PJ wrapped her arms around the frail woman for a moment, knowing how much grief she was still feeling over Timmy. Before PJ walked into the study, she asked, "May I use the powder room upstairs?"

Connie gestured toward the back of the walnut paneled study. "No need to go upstairs. I'm sure James wouldn't object if you used his private facilities. Now if you will excuse me, I must return to my work upstairs."

PJ managed a smile, watching her retreat from the room. She knew the "work" upstairs was her constant vigil in Timmy's room.

PJ left the door to the study open so she could hear Joshua, if he came in while she was in the bathroom. Ever since she walked out on him at the Varsity, they had not spoken and she wanted to patch things up. She felt it better to do so at his home.

Now, she stood in front of the mirror over the black marble vanity, touching up her lipstick as she thought about Joshua.

Her thoughts were interrupted by a shouting, angry voice in the study. She recognized the voice of Dr. Smith conversing with someone on the telephone. Unsure what to do, she remained quiet, unable to avoid eavesdropping.

"Ortega, I told you I can handle the situation here but I need more people. Weber has his hands full running the dealers. I need someone who can take over that responsibility and free Weber up for security."

PJ covered her mouth to stifle a gasp. Silence in the adjacent room meant Dr. Smith was now listening to this person on the phone. Why would Dr. Smith say, "Weber was busy running the dealers?" Why would he know such a man?

He spoke again, his voice breaking. "I told you the last time we met; I have no idea who is muscling in. My people swear there are no new dealers on the streets. No Asians or Cubans. I have a man on the inside at police headquarters and he swears the police are just as mystified. They don't have a clue what's happening!"

PJ's knees buckled when she heard the last remark. From the brief conversation she had overheard, there was no doubt Dr. Smith was into drug trafficking. She needed to sit down and, reaching for the toilet seat, her hand brushed against a small vessel of potpourri. The ceramic container crashed to the floor, shattering on the tile.

The voice from the study ceased, followed by whispering, and then silence again.

The door to the bathroom was jerked open and Smith stepped into the small room with a large handgun aimed at PJ's head. "This is most unfortunate, young lady. Now, you just come along quietly or I'll drag you. Either way, you are leaving this house, now!"

Her legs trembled as she walked across the study into the foyer, followed by Smith. She said a silent prayer, hoping Joshua would come in or Connie would appear on the stairs. Neither happened.

Smith pushed her through the kitchen and out the door to the adjoining garage. He opened the trunk of the Mercedes, motioning for PJ to climb into the small compartment.

She knew to do so would mean her death, so she screamed and bolted for the door back into the kitchen. She reached it, one hand searching for the door knob, the other fighting to break free from Dr. Smith. She pulled from his grasp, grabbed the metal knob and as the door swung open, her world turned black.

The traffic was sparse on the Athens/Jefferson bypass. Shadows from the tall pine trees that stretched along the pastures were gone by the time Smith arrived at the turnoff to Weber's place. The sedan's high beams played across tree trunks and small shrubs as the car bounced down the dirt road, negotiating the frequent sharp turns with ease.

A long day had become a bad day as well when Smith received the unexpected call from Weber. Smith was reluctant to change his plans and risk unwanted questions but Weber had been insistent, spouting off about an emergency situation that couldn't be discussed on the phone. Finally he relented, but told Weber that a price would be paid for the inconvenience and unnecessary exposure.

Arriving at the back of the cabin, Smith encountered Weber's thugs posted outside. He made a weak protest during the security pat-down but balked when they attempted to take his wallet. He was pleased, however, to see some semblance of organization by Weber. It was an improvement over Manuel's ineptitude.

"Back off, he's okay." Weber stood at the top of the steps to a small wooden back porch with a waist-high rail. A tall overweight Caucasian was standing to the left of Weber.

Smith recognized Pete by the wimpy mustache that did little to hide a botched attempt to repair a cleft lip. Smith flushed in anger at the obvious security breach. Pete was not cleared to know his identity.

"Weber, why is this person here?"

Weber ignored the question, gesturing with both hands in the air. "We got bad problems, boss. We learned it's a bunch of kids that's fucking with us."

Smith continued to stare at Pete, who gawked in surprise at the person Weber called "boss."

"What the hell are you talking about?" Smith asked Weber. "I don't believe a bunch of kids are wasting our people. It has to be professionals who are trying to take over our territory, and you're not doing a thing about it, holing up out here."

Weber turned his head to the side and let fly a wad of tobacco-stained mucus. He didn't like being taken to task by anyone other than Ortega. "I don't spend all my time here. I do all the transfers since the truck got busted, plus play nurse maid to all the dealers."

Smith motioned for the other two to precede him into the small cabin. "We'll discuss that matter later. Why did you get me out here, and I repeat, what the hell is he doing here?"

Weber's face flushed and Pete spoke up. "Rafael, one of our street dealers, set up a kid to meet me. The kid said he knew me through Carlos, and said he was a friend of your dead son and wanted to make a big score. When I told Weber about the meeting, he got worried. We picked up the kid and brought him here to find out what he was after, since he never bought anything before."

Smith turned toward Weber. "Why does this person know about me and my son? You know the rules of security we set up. No one should know my name and involvement except you. Did Ortega not make his instructions clear enough for you? It looks like you are in way over your head."

In spite of the cool evening air, sweat rolled off Weber's face, dripping onto his massive chest. He swallowed hard. "Boss, I had no choice. After the truck bust, I had to get someone local involved to help check up on the dealers. We had to make sure no one was turning on us. Pete knows all the dealers, even those who were capped. His brother-in-law is that Hispanic kid, Carlos, the one who sold the drugs to your son. Pete's working with me to see if Carlos is pulling some shit on us. He might be the one contaminating our supply. Pete knows his stuff and can be trusted."

Smith looked at Pete for a moment before making eye contact with Weber. "You better be a good judge of character. You are staking your life on his trustworthiness."

Weber blurted out, "My boys got the kid to talk. It took some persuasion but he decided to talk after they knocked out his teeth and broke both kneecaps. He told us plenty, but you won't like what we learned. You made a good decision not wasting that bitch at your cabin."

Smith blanched, trying to connect the useless crap Weber was blabbering to his incarceration of PJ. "What are you talking about? What has the girl got to do with this kid you brought out here?"

"The kid told us your son Joshua is the one who's making all the big buys. He's also the guy who was dealing directly with Manuel, before he got zapped."

Smith's face turned ashen. "The kid is lying. No way is Joshua mixed up in drugs." Even as he spoke, he remembered how much Joshua had changed over the past months. He realized it might be credible.

"Where is the kid? I want to question him personally."

Weber stared at Pete, avoiding eye contact with Smith. "Fuck me, can't do it. Pete and the boys got a little too rough. The kid's dead."

Smith exploded in rage. "Goddamn you, Weber. Can't you do anything right? How are we going to know if he was telling the truth? He would have told you anything if he thought it would save his life."

Smith paced the floor, rubbing the back of his neck to ease the throbbing tension headache. "If Joshua is involved, the girl has information. Weber, your men can look after this place. Get your ass to my cabin and stay there until I get back to you. Pete, go back to Athens and keep your mouth shut. No dealing for now. Any of the street punks start asking questions, tell them the supplies are temporarily low. If Joshua gets in touch with you, put him off but do not meet with him. You understand?"

Pete nodded.

Weber appeared hesitant to speak. He looked toward the front of the cabin before turning back to Smith. "Uh ... what do we do with the kid's body?"

Smith returned a cold stare. "I don't care. Just make sure it disappears or there will be two more bodies for me to worry about."

Weber didn't need further clarification.

Smith turned to leave, paused and looked at Pete. "Who was the kid you picked up?"

"Called himself Eddie," Pete said.

Smith walked toward his car. He remembered Eddie as the boy with Timmy on the night he died. "Another loser," he muttered.

The edge of darkness crept over his neighborhood as Joshua drove down Dogwood Trail. He shrugged his shoulders, the muscles sore from the practice that had extended into the night hours. Deep in thought over his rift with PJ, he allowed his attention to drift and swerved just in time to miss a decorative brick and iron mailbox.

With the game with Georgia Tech a week away, he had struggled to stay focused at practice. Twice during passing drills he was called to the sideline, replaced by the backup quarterback. The coaches didn't say a word to him; it wasn't necessary. Just pulling him was enough to send a message to him and his teammates that unless his performance improved, he would not start the game against Tech.

His mood perked up at the sight of PJ's Honda Accord parked at his home. His heart pounded with excitement. For the first time in days, he felt elated.

He wheeled into the circular drive and jumped from the Jeep toward the house, racing up the steps, taking two at a time. Entering the foyer, he called out her name. When she didn't answer, he checked the kitchen, and the den. He peered into the back yard; the pool deck and the gazebo were deserted. When he walked back into the kitchen he heard his mother call out.

"Joshua, PJ came by earlier to see you. She was waiting in your father's study but that was hours ago. I'm sure she's gone by now."

He saw his mother standing at the top of the stairs—still in the clothes she had worn at breakfast. With a forced cheerfulness, he responded. "Thanks, Mom. Her car is outside. She may have fallen asleep on Dad's sofa. I'll check on her." The smile mustered for his mother's sake disappeared when he saw her retreat into Timmy's room. He felt helpless over his inability to reach through her pain and comfort her.

Joshua eased the door open to the study, not wanting to startle PJ if she was asleep. He frowned as he canvassed the empty room. The door to the half bath was open, something his father wouldn't do. Joshua called again, walking toward the bathroom. "PJ?"

When he didn't hear a response he pulled the door all the way open and peered in. He saw the broken ceramic and potpourri scattered across the floor. He stepped into the small room, noticing PJ's purse on the vanity. He picked it up, carrying it with him as he left the study and climbed the carpeted steps to the second level. As expected, he found his mother at Timmy's desk, looking through his old homework papers.

He fought the urge to retreat, entering the room. "Mom, PJ wasn't in the study, but I found her purse in the bathroom." He didn't mention the broken container. "Has Dad been home today?"

His mother looked up with a blank stare. "I don't think so. He went to a meeting with the members of the medical mission group. They are planning another trip to Colombia."

Joshua shook his head angrily. "I can't believe it. We need him here more than the people of Colombia. It's not fair to you or me."

He realized his words were lost on his mother's deaf ears; she had returned to her private world of grief.

He decided to check PJ's car in case she left a note, but even as he thought of the possibility he couldn't explain why she had left her purse in the bathroom.

When he didn't find a note, he returned to the house, his mind filled with anguish, puzzlement and anger. "What the hell is going on?" he questioned the empty study.

CHAPTER 35

Joshua parked in the back lot of the Varsity. He climbed out of the Jeep when he saw Calvin pull in and park a few spaces away. With deliberate steps Joshua walked to the car, trying hard to control his anger.

He had received a message on his cell phone earlier, but Calvin after identifying himself had stammered so badly, Joshua was only able to decipher "Varsity at noon."

Joshua sat down in the passenger seat, slamming the car door. "Okay, tell me what is going on. I can tell by the strained look on your face that you and Eddie are up to something. It will get worse if you don't tell me now."

Calvin's chin dropped to his chest. His heart thumped against his sternum as he tried to speak. "I'm scared, Joshua. I know we shouldn't have done it. You told us not to do anything, but Eddie insisted and I helped."

Joshua yelled at him, "What the hell are you talking about? Start from the beginning and tell me everything the two of you have done. Maybe I can help. Where is Eddie?"

"I … I … I don't know," Calvin answered, stuttering worse than ever in his panic. "I took him to the K Mart parking lot Saturday night for a meeting with Pete. I didn't stay there because he didn't want me around. I was to pick him up at eleven but when I went back, he wasn't there. I waited until two in the morning but he never showed up. I had to go home. I thought he would call me Sunday, but I haven't heard from him since."

Joshua pressed his eyes with the heels of both hands, trying to ward off the sudden stab of pain he felt. The nagging fear that the young kids would do something and get in over their heads had come true; now Eddie might have paid a high price for his bravado.

"How did Eddie contact Pete? He's never met Pete. I told both of you to stay away from the dealers."

Calvin's eyes were brimming with tears. "He got Rafael to set it up—we couldn't find Carlos. Eddie just wanted to help you. We both do."

Joshua sensed the truth in Calvin's words, making the situation even harder to take. His quest for revenge had involved the boys, and even though he had warned them and kept them isolated from actual contact with the dealers, whatever happened to them was his doing.

In his mind's eye he could visualize the horrors Eddie might be facing. If they harmed Eddie, his plans would change. Even if it cost him his career, even his life, he would forget about getting the detectives involved. He would hunt down every dealer he could, get them isolated and kill them.

"Go home, Calvin. Tell no one about this. Let me handle it and stay away from Rafael."

Joshua walked from the field house toward the players' parking lot. With his mind on Eddie's disappearance, football practice had been a disaster. When he saw the beige sedan adjacent to his Jeep, he said goodbye to the teammates who were walking with him and stomped toward the familiar car.

"Is this 'harass Joshua Smith week' again?"

Anderson and Billings got out of the sedan and moved together to the front of Joshua's Jeep. They said nothing as they leaned against the hood and stared at Joshua.

"What is it?" Joshua said, directing his question to Anderson.

"You tell us. We've been talking with Missing Persons and it seems another one of your friends is missing. His parents reported he went out a few nights ago and hasn't returned home. It's not likely he's a runaway."

"Who are you talking about?"

"Eddie Hubbard. I'm sure you remember Eddie. Your brother's friend who was with him at the lake the night your brother died. And from recent information from Eddie's friend, Calvin Jenkins, you have become rather close to Eddie yourself."

Joshua tossed his backpack in the passenger seat of his Jeep. "So I befriended Eddie. Why question me about his missing status?"

"Just thought you might know something. Maybe he told you about a trip he was taking. Maybe he decided to go look for your girlfriend since she's still missing and you don't appear to be too upset about it. We told Calvin to be careful; it's not a good idea to be too close to you right now."

Joshua moved toward Anderson but was cut off by Billings.

"You don't want to tangle with my partner," Billings said. "He might be smaller than you but he's a real Tasmanian devil when he's pissed and, believe me, he's pissed."

Joshua backed away but shouted in Anderson's face, "I hate your guts, Detective Anderson. You've got a bee up your ass about me and you're making it a campaign to drive me nuts. I'm hurting enough over the disappearance of my fiancée. I don't need your continuous harassment. I don't know where you get your information but I've talked to PJ's sorority sisters, her professors, and her parents, and I have no clue where she has gone. As I told you before, I don't know why her car was at my house and no one in our neighborhood saw her. So why don't you spend your time looking for her and leave me alone."

Billings gave his partner a tap on the shoulder and they returned to their car. Without another word they entered and drove away.

Joshua climbed into his Jeep, inserted the key but didn't start the engine. He covered his face with his hands and sobbed.

Two blocks away Billings drove the sedan onto the edge of the road, turned off the engine and looked at his partner. "Well, Sherlock, what do you think?"

"I think he's up to his neck in something, I just don't know what. But I've got my teeth in his ass now and I'm not letting up."

Billings cranked the engine and pulled back on the road. "Just be careful. His old man swings a lot of weight in Athens and can bring trouble down on you in a hurry."

"That's why I got you, partner. To fend off my troubles."

CHAPTER 36

Joshua lay on his bed staring at the swirled patterns on his plastered ceiling. His mind was in a similar state, going in circles with no forward movement. His anxiety over PJ's disappearance was now compounded by the apparent abduction of Eddie. Was it possible the two events were related? How could they be?

He could think only of PJ and how to find her. The longer he withheld the information he possessed from the police, the less the chance of finding PJ alive. He mentally sorted through the different scenarios he could present to the detectives. There had to be a way he could tell them what he knew without incriminating himself, and making them even more suspicious. The thought of retribution from Weber caused him little concern; Weber would have no way of knowing how the detectives got the information.

The possibility that Weber and Pete had nothing to do with the disappearance of PJ entered his mind, but he dismissed it. The thing that troubled him the most was it appeared she had disappeared from his own house. Had Weber been watching for him and grabbed PJ to use as leverage?

The electric-powered garage door opened. It had to be his father; his mother never left the house. He had some questions to ask his father. He was troubled over the lack of attention his mother was receiving. Her mental state was getting worse each day and his father showed little concern. He knew his father to be a proud man, but, damn his pride, it was time to get Mom the professional help she needed even if it caused a rift between him and his father.

Joshua hurried down the stairs in his socks to meet his father when he came into the kitchen from the garage. He was surprised to see the door to the study swing closed just as he stepped into the foyer. He knocked on the door a couple of times; no response. He attempted to turn the knob but the door was locked, so he knocked louder. Finally, he heard his father's voice.

"Yes, who is it?"

"Sorry to disturb you, Dad. May I come in? I need to talk to you."

"Not at the moment, Joshua. I've got several things to do and I need to return to the hospital in a few minutes. Check with me after I get back. I should be home before eleven."

Joshua raised his fist to pound on the door but changed his mind. Aware of his father's unusual behavior lately, he decided not to push things until he returned from his evening rounds so they would have adequate time to discuss things. He returned to his room to try and study while he waited for his father's return.

When he heard the garage door open a second time, he returned to the kitchen. Looking out the window, he saw the Mercedes exit the driveway. He was surprised when the big sedan drove off in the opposite direction from the hospital.

Joshua returned to his room and sat on the floor, his legs crossed under him. Everything he saw around him reminded him of PJ—her picture on the dresser, the banner on the wall she had made for one of his games, the Peachtree Road Race tee shirt he earned when he and PJ ran the 10K race. He pulled his knees up to his chest, wrapped his arms around them and leaned back against the bed. His head dropped forward; his forehead touching his knees.

She had to be alive, somewhere. Even if she was unhappy in their relationship, she wouldn't just leave and put her parents through the agony they were enduring.

He was certain there was no other man in her life; they were too close even if they often disagreed on things. He had been too preoccupied; maybe he had missed important signs; maybe she had been trying to reach him and couldn't. He was desperate to find her but had exhausted all that he knew to do. His selfish quest for revenge had possibly cost the life of Eddie, and now maybe PJ's life as well.

He slid over to the bedside table, removing a letter from the top drawer. The letter was from PJ and had arrived the day after she disappeared. He had read it so many times, he had memorized the words.

"My darling, Joshua. This is not a 'Dear John' letter as I am not leaving your life for good, but I think we need some space for a while until you decide what is most important for you. You've been with me so seldom and when we are together, your mind is always somewhere else. You've lost your enthusiasm for sports and your studies. I know you love me, but I am way down the list of your priorities. I think you lost sight of our future and are dwelling too much on the past. No matter what you do, you can't bring Timmy back. If something terrible should happen to you, it would be the final blow to your mother. I love you more than anything in the world but I can not be with you and watch you destroy yourself. I realize we will see each other at classes but unless you separate yourself from your obsession, please do not speak to me. This is like a death but maybe time will heal our wounds. I love you, PJ."

Joshua dropped the letter in his lap, burying his face in his hands. The first time he had read the letter, he was angry at PJ for being so selfish. Now he saw things from her perspective and understood her feelings. She had come to his house to plead with him again, but for some reason she never got the chance. Whatever happened to her, he felt responsible.

Joshua pushed up from the floor, wiped his eyes and started downstairs. He wanted to look around the study again, maybe he overlooked a note. The police failed to find anything but he would look again. At least it was something to do.

The door to the study was locked again. He remembered times during his childhood when he would go into the study and play with his toy cars on the carpeted floor while his father read his medical journals. The door was never locked in those days.

He knocked, but there was no response. He started back upstairs but became curious why his father remained cloistered in the study all night when he was at home.

He retrieved a thin fillet knife from the kitchen and with a little effort was able to jimmy the lock by sliding the knife between the door facing and the lock. Entering the room, he was shocked at the disorder. This was unusual. Several file boxes were stacked on the desk top and others were on the floor in front of the credenza.

Curious as to what his father was working on so hard, Joshua began rummaging through the boxes. At first he thought the papers were information on medical mission trips since so much of the data pertained to Colombia. Further reading made that possibility unlikely. Names, places and shipping receipts did not coincide with his trips. Invoices for shipments of ceramic figurines were made out to Ortega Import in Atlanta. His father's name was nowhere on the invoices but his signature was at the bottom of each page.

Other boxes revealed similar information along with financial data from an accounting firm, also located in Atlanta. The data was again directed to Ortega Import with his father listed as one of the directors.

Joshua had never heard his father mention the company or anything about being in the import business.

He relocked the door when he left, his mind flooded with information he could not interpret. How did any of this fit in with PJ's disappearance?

CHAPTER 37

Abandoned warehouses that heralded the days when cotton was king overlooked the river that snaked through the south side of Athens. The warehouses now featured shattered windows broken by vandals, huge gaps in the tin roofs and wooden doors barely hanging on their rusty hinges.

Carlos stood in the shadow of the second building in the chain, awaiting the right moment to move up to the street. His truck was parked several blocks away. He preferred to be on his feet if things went wrong. It would be easier to disappear among the abandoned buildings than outrun anyone in his truck.

He glanced at his watch, noted the time and moved out of the shadows. His timing was perfect. When he arrived at the roadside, Joshua's Jeep pulled alongside. Carlos jumped in and barely got the door closed before Joshua gunned the engine, slinging gravel and dirt.

"Damn, amigo. I almost lost a leg back there. Take it easy. Not need to be in such a hurry."

"Yes, we do. Eddie didn't come back from a meeting with Pete. Rafael set it up and Calvin took Eddie to the meeting. When Calvin went back for the arranged pickup, Eddie never showed up and hasn't been seen since. I tried to find you. I thought maybe you could help but it was like you had disappeared as well."

Carlos shook his head in sorrow. "I had to. I was caught in the middle. I did not know Rafael set it up. If they got Eddie, he is already dead. They would torture him until he told them what they wanted to know and then they would kill him. They would never let him go."

Joshua was silent a moment and then glanced over at Carlos. "Have you heard anything at all about PJ? I feel bad even asking the question because I'm sure you would have told me if you did, but I'm desperate."

"I know what you must feel, but I stay away from everybody and I don't know anything. I am sorry for you. I really worry about what Eddie might have told them. No matter how brave he try to be they would learn everything. If he told Pete about me setting up meetings for you, then I need to become invisible. Or, maybe there is something better."

Everything around Pete moved faster than normal, or so it seemed. He liked his booze, but seldom did drugs—but these were not ordinary times. Since the events at Weber's cabin, he had been unsettled, not only from the threats he received, but also from the knowledge of the MAN.

Who would have believed one of the most respected doctors in town was the leader of the drug ring? It concerned him that he knew such information. Smith might become apprehensive and decide there were too many loose ends. Pete didn't like being a "loose end." He reached into the baggie, removing the last pinch of the magic powder.

As he drove through the streets the cocaine made him feel invincible. He didn't like the idea of staying away from the street guys. He had worked hard setting up his own links and if he cut these guys off, they would be gone in a couple of weeks. It might be okay for Smith to cut off his own cash flow from the drugs but Pete didn't have any income source other than the drugs and was dependent on the day-to-day cash flow. This was a bad fucking time to lay low.

He continued to cruise the streets, eyeballing some of the dealers, but didn't stop. Too many witnesses around; Smith might have his own spies out. He cursed Smith under his breath, continuing to meander through the downtown streets.

Joshua drove slowly around the south side. "Are you sure Pete's out here tonight?"

"He is here somewhere. He needs money and without me to handle his deals, he will have to find his own action. Just keep driving around. He will spot your Jeep sooner or later and when he sees us together, he will follow us."

Joshua was in his own world when he turned at the next intersection and met Pete going in the opposite direction. He didn't notice but Carlos did.

"Keep going. Pete just drove past us and I am sure he saw us. Yes, he's turning around and is about one hundred feet behind us."

Joshua increased the speed and drove up West Broad Street, turned on Oglethorpe and followed it to Tallassee Road. After traveling under the Athens Bypass he turned again on White Creek Road into the wooded section across the small tributary from Bishop Park. He accelerated to increase the distance between the vehicles, swung left and, when he lost sight of Pete's car in the rear-view mirror, he slowed long enough for Carlos to bail out of the passenger side of the Jeep into some brush. He continued on for another fifty yards, did a U-turn and headed back. When he reached the area of his previous left turn the road was blocked by Pete's vehicle.

Joshua jumped out of the Jeep. Taking the offensive, he stormed toward Pete's car.

When Pete saw Joshua running toward him, he flipped open his glove compartment and withdrew his .38 Police Special. He rested the barrel on the edge of the open window, aimed at Joshua, who skidded to a stop at the driver's door.

Ignoring the gun, Joshua yelled, "Where's Eddie, you bastard?"

Pete extended the pistol further out the window. "I don't know what you're talking about."

"Like hell, you don't. Calvin told me that Eddie was meeting you at K Mart and when he went back to pick him up, he wasn't there. No one has seen him since."

"Well, that's too bad. To tell you the truth, I killed the little punk. He wasn't as tough as he thought; didn't like my knife too much. Squealed like a pig when I carved out his balls. Now, where is Carlos? I saw the little shit in the Jeep with you."

Joshua moved toward the side mirror, resting his arm against it. "You are seeing things. Must be the guilt you feel for the way you've treated Carlos. I would like to beat you to death with my bare hands but we're taking you to the police. I'll bet they can make you squeal like a pig as well."

Pete spat out his words. "Go to hell, you privileged prick. You are going to join your hot little girl friend."

Pete threw his weight against the door just as he yanked hard on the handle. The heavy door swung open, striking Joshua, who had not anticipated the move. He pitched backwards, landing hard on his right shoulder.

Pete leaped from the car, leveling the pistol at him. "So you were going to take me to the police."

From behind Pete came a familiar voice. "He said 'we,' idiot."

Pete attempted to swing his gun around but he wasn't quick enough. Two hammering blows struck him in the center of his back, the bullets exiting through his chest, taking most of the heart with them.

Blood and tissue splattered Joshua, who was scrambling backwards on the road. "Goddamn!" he cried out. "Carlos, what the fuck?"

Carlos shoved the .357 Magnum back into his belt, pulling his jacket over it. "This is not a game for me, Joshua." He looked down at Pete, then back at Joshua. With little emotion he said, "He's not the first. Take me back to my truck."

Joshua got to his feet, breathless, his heart racing. "You ... you are the killer of the dealers?"

"Not by myself. At first Rafael worked alone because they got his sister hooked and turned her into a street whore. I joined him after Pete killed Timmy. Now, let's get out of here."

Joshua was shaking. "But Pete—Pete knew something about PJ!"

"Sorry. Pete gave me no choice. If he knew something he not tell you. I would have killed him anyway."

Joshua began to have doubts about his decision to live at home. The coaching staff had made an unusual exception for him so he could be close to his mother, but being alone all the time made things worse. The scene with Pete replayed over and over in his mind. What did Pete know? Oh God! If only Carlos hadn't reacted so quickly.

As Joshua stared at his class notes on his desk, his mind pictured PJ as she looked the night they sat together in the gazebo.

A second trip to the police headquarters with PJ's parents had been futile, with no new information regarding her disappearance. The authorities had impounded her Honda and searched and fingerprinted it thoroughly but came up empty. He couldn't cast stones at the police for the lack of progress since he was withholding vital clues. He had not told them about finding PJ's purse or the broken container. His poor mother was now so mentally out of it she didn't remember that PJ had been to the house.

Joshua slammed his book on top of the spiral notebook, sending his pen sailing across the room. He was growing despondent over his inability to tie up all the loose ends. Why had PJ disappeared from his house? What had his progress in his personal investigation come to such a screeching halt? And why wouldn't Detective Anderson leave him alone?

He pushed back from his desk, so distracted he decided to forego the attempt at studying for a few minutes. He had never been one for study groups and with his mother so ill, he had chosen to stay at home as much as possible. The coaches approved his request as long as he attended practice and maintained a self-imposed curfew. As far as they knew, he did. He attended classes regularly but got a break on his required lab work since he had a perfect 4.0 in chemistry.

He walked to the kitchen to make a sandwich and to get a Coke. When he passed the window in the breakfast nook he saw Anderson's car parked at the end of the driveway. He slammed his fist on the kitchen counter in anger. This was nothing more than more harassment. If Anderson needed more information concerning PJ, then why didn't he call or at least come to the front door. But no, all he did was sit in his car in the driveway for a few minutes and then drive away. Not the first time.

Giving up on any worthwhile studying, Joshua grabbed his coat and the offensive playbook for the Georgia Tech game and left for practice.

His quest was becoming a nightmare and his accomplishments were pitifully lean compared to the cost.

The atmosphere in Sanford Stadium was festive and charged with anticipation of a good old-fashioned slug fest. The weather was perfect, a brisk forty-five degrees, very little wind and most important of all— no rain.

Georgia Tech had a mediocre season of seven wins and three losses, well below their standards. But as most of the old-timers would tell you—"You can throw out the records when it comes to any Tech/Georgia game." The members of both squads played the game for state bragging rights and performed as it were for the national championship. Tech had no aspirations of a national title but Georgia was still in the hunt with a perfect ten wins and no losses. Win against Tech and then beat LSU in the SEC Conference Championship game, and they would retain their number two ranking in the BCS and would have a shot at the national title against Southern California, presently number one in the nation. First, Georgia had to get by Tech.

Joshua clapped his hands and stomped his feet in an attempt to disperse some of his nervous energy. He stood in the tunnel leading from the dressing room with his teammates all around him. Pregame instructions and prayers were completed and the players patiently awaited the signal from the officials to run onto the field.

Television gave the teams a lot of exposure and accounted for a large portion of revenue earned by the football programs. At the same time it was sometimes a pain in the ass, like now. The game had been moved back to eight o'clock in the evening to accommodate the networks desire of a prime time game but the extra wait created more tension for Joshua and the others.

Finally the signal came and he led the team through throngs of screaming fans to the home team sideline. The players on both sides of the field began pounding their teammates on the shoulder pads, grabbing face masks and generally behaved like gladiators about to enter the Roman Coliseum.

The partisan crowd went wild when the Bulldogs won the toss and were driven to a frenzy when the Georgia player caught the kickoff deep in the end zone and brought it out in a burst up the middle to the Georgia forty-five yard line. Two quick handoffs on slant plays and the ball rested at Tech's thirty-four with less than two minutes gone off the clock.

Joshua called a play and the team broke the huddle. He looked over the defense, noting the strong safety up near the line of scrimmage. Blitz, Joshua thought. He motioned for the running back to move up in a blocking position behind the right offensive tackle. The ball was snapped and Joshua took a three-step drop-back. The strong safety didn't blitz, he dropped back into pass coverage but the middle linebacker charged through the line taking advantage of the offensive lines misdirection.

Joshua rolled out to his right but the running lanes were blocked by the outside linebacker and the defensive end who shifted toward the sideline. The middle linebacker changed directions and pursued Joshua toward the out of bounds line.

Joshua looked downfield. The wide receiver was covered. The slot receiver from the left side dropped off his route and moved toward the center of the field. In desperation Joshua launched a high pass just as he was driven into the turf by the middle linebacker. He didn't see the strong safety slide into the pattern and intercept the ball but the groans from the fans said it all.

Joshua got up, brushed off grass and sod jammed into his facemask and trotted across the field to his own sideline. He was met by the offensive coach.

"What in the hell were you thinking, Smith? You never throw late back across the middle. We just lost a chance to score on the opening drive against a damn good defense."

Joshua lowered his head and sought a spot on the bench next to the center.

The remainder of the first half did not improve. Both teams were guilty of a series of errors—fumbles, interceptions and penalties. At the end of the first half the teams went to their respective locker rooms to a smattering of applause from a less than enthusiastic crowd.

Joshua glanced up at the scoreboard at the 3-3 score as if he needed a reminder of the anemic play of the team and himself. The coaches had encouraged, pleaded and then cursed the players to perform up to their level of competence. Nothing seemed to work.

The coaches were relatively silent in the locker room. A few of the position coaches spoke quietly to individual players but there was no loud harangue from the head coach. No speeches were needed. The defense had played an excellent first half. Everyone in the room knew where the problem lay.

Joshua sat on a stool staring at his hands. When an official notified the team to head out for the field there was no fired-up yelling or screaming. Joshua remained on the stool, and as the players filed out, each of them gave him a pat on the shoulder. He couldn't look at them. He was devastated and tears filled his eyes. He was letting them down. He had been their leader all season long, and now for a reason that had nothing to do with them he was incapable of being their leader.

After the last of the players left the room Joshua put on his helmet and followed. When he reached the entrance to the tunnel he came face to face with the quarterback coach, the man who showed more faith in him than anyone.

Reality overcame ego. "I don't have it, coach. I don't know what's wrong," he lied, "but I just can't get it done."

The coach nodded. "You just showed me why you will always be a good leader. Don't worry about it. If the defense can continue their stellar play and keep Tech out of the end zone, I think Franklin can pull it out for us. It won't help us in the polls but a win is a win. Just try to get yourself together before the LSU game. We'll need you at one hundred percent for that game."

The defense were indeed the heroes of the game as they not only prevented Tech from scoring, but Jerry Drath, a Bulldog cornerback, intercepted a pass in the fourth quarter and ran it back eighty yards for the only touchdown of the game. The Bulldogs pulled out a victory. 10-3.

Afterwards, to a man, every player filed by Joshua's locker with a kind word or gesture. His pain was evident and he knew the coaches and players assumed it must be due to PJ's disappearance.

It was almost two o'clock in the morning before Joshua left the building. He spoke briefly to a maintenance staff member before starting his lonely walk to the parking lot. He had become a pariah and everyone who loved him, suffered.

CHAPTER 38

Concealed in a thicket of tall pine trees on a hillside overlooking Lake Hartwell was an isolated log cabin. The structure was the only one on either side of a tongue of water splitting two rolling hills. The windows of the cabin were covered with heavy shutters. The lone entrance was through a heavy oak door at the front of the building. A stacked field stone chimney, absent of smoke, graced the back. To a casual observer, the place looked deserted.

PJ lay on her side in a double bed, one arm manacled to an iron bed post. She had lost track of time but estimated fifteen days had passed since Dr. Smith dumped her in the cabin.

He had not returned.

Instead, a man who smelled of garlic and sweat had initially entered the bedroom three times a day to carry her to the bathroom, still gagged and with hood in place. She was shocked the first time the man jerked off her sweats and pulled down her bikini panties. Though she couldn't see him, she imagined his evil smile as he watched her urinate. Once he had put his hand between her legs as if to wipe her, but she head-butted him and he did not attempt it again.

On the third day of captivity her menses started, and her capturer evidently decided not to deal with the problem. The visits were increased to four times a day and her legs were left unbound. She was led to the bathroom and manacled by one wrist to a heavy chain imbedded in a large block of cement. The chain was of sufficient length to allow her to use the commode and the lavatory but not long enough for her to reach the small window near the ceiling. The horrid man even provided sanitary napkins though she refused his offer to help her use them.

She was warned in no uncertain terms not to attempt to cry out for help. If she did, the gag and hood would go back in place. She obeyed her instructions and prolonged her visits to the bathroom as long as she could. Looking at the sunshine through the permanently sealed window helped keep her from going insane.

After the fourth day the man had tired of her constant pleading and removed the hood and gag that previously were removed only for meals and when she went to the bathroom. Other than the discomfort of the bindings, and suffering the voyeurism, she was not harmed nor questioned. No one saw her leave the Smiths' home, nor would they have any idea where she was. In all the years she had been with Joshua, he had never mentioned this cabin and likely was unaware of its existence. Her only solace was prayer, so she prayed for her life, for Joshua, Connie, and even for Dr. Smith.

PJ maneuvered her legs to a position to gain leverage so she could sit up with her back against the head board. She heard the front door open, followed by two voices in conversation. She returned to her previous position, lying on her side with her face toward the bedroom door to hear the voices better. The muffled sounds became louder. The speakers were approaching the bedroom.

The door opened with the familiar squeak she had heard so many times before. She remained in her reclined position but opened her eyes. She saw Dr. Smith peering at her as if she was one of his seriously ill patients in the ICU.

"How are you doing, Pamela?"

PJ clenched her jaws. She wanted to tell him to go to hell, to stop his pompous formality, but in spite of her sense of bravado, she whispered, "Please let me go home. My parents must be worried to death. I promise I won't say anything about what I heard or where I've been."

"I would like to let you go home right now, but that's not possible until I have a talk with Joshua. How much does he know about my business affairs?"

PJ heard snickering in the background but it stopped when Smith cleared his throat.

"Joshua? He doesn't know anything," she said. "I didn't know anything until I overheard you in your office. I wasn't spying. I was just using the bathroom while I waited for Joshua to come home." In spite of her attempt to be brave, she broke down.

"Please let me go home. I don't care what you do. Just let me go home to my mom and dad. Promise me you won't hurt Joshua."

"That, my dear, depends on Joshua. It appears he's been involved in activities that could lead to serious trouble for all of us."

"What are you talking about?"

Smith remained silent. After a long pause he shook his head in resignation and left the room.

A long period of silence was broken by the sound of the closing front door. PJ sobbed on the bed, her entire body shaking from fear and frustration. For the first time she understood; she would never see home again.

CHAPTER 39

A momentary quiet in the police station downtown was shattered by a steady streak of four-letter words aimed at two patrolmen dragging a man into the bull pen. The sergeant on duty at the outer desk looked up at the intoxicated college student and added his own barrage of obscenities.

Carlos sat in one corner of the room doing his best to remain unnoticed. Instinct told him to bolt from the place, but he was smart enough to realize Anderson would find him and make his life even more miserable. He had been near the bus terminal when he was picked up by a patrol car, brought to the station and deposited on the wooden bench. He had been told in clear understandable language not to move. For the past four hours he watched the circus of actors brought into the station, each loudly claiming police cruelty and their own innocence.

He was unconcerned about the pick-up. He was clean and the patrolmen knew that he was never violent. They treated him okay. He was a regular, picked up by the same guys whenever a general rousting was ordered by their superiors.

Anderson entered, ambling across the room while he munched on an apple, his belated lunch. He motioned for Carlos to join him as he exited the building.

Anderson squatted on the granite steps at the front of the station, waving Carlos to a spot beside him. He finished the apple and pitched the remaining core into the bushes adjacent to the steps.

"I've got bad news for you," he said.

Sweat broke out in small beads across Carlos' face. This was the news he dreaded; his cooperation had not helped. They were going to deport him.

Anderson continued, "We found the body of your brother-in-law this morning. He was back shot. I don't guess you know anything about that?"

Anderson watched Carlos' head slump on his chest, so he remained silent for a few moments.

Carlos was hiding his emotions, suppressing a grin that the news was not about his deportation.

"I know nothing about it. I not see him for days."

Anderson put a stick of Big Red gum in his mouth and offered one to Carlos, who declined. "Best we can tell, he was killed sometime last night. Do you know why he was on White Creek Road? Did he mention plans to meet someone?"

"Pete never tell me his plans. He just told me what to do." Carlos paused, then asked, "Does my sister know?"

Anderson nodded. "A female officer took a social worker to her house soon after we identified the body. They attempted to get information but your sister didn't know anything other than Pete left about ten last night and didn't come home."

Carlos stared at the pavement for a full minute before he looked up at Anderson. "I'm glad he's dead."

"I know he gave you a hard time and I believe what you told me before. Pete got you involved in the drug business against your will. You keep helping us and we'll see that you and your sister are taken care of in a proper fashion."

"Just take care of my sister. I will take care of Carlos."

CHAPTER 40

A fine line exists between sanity and insanity; Joshua was straddling that line. His plans were going awry as if some invisible force was working against him. At the moment those evil spirits were invading his head; dancing stars and flashing lights were at the periphery of his vision along with worsening nausea, a sure sign of an impending migraine headache. He grabbed a couple of Excedrin Migraine from the bathroom cabinet, washing them down with gulps of water from the lavatory. The strain of PJ's disappearance was taking its toll.

His football life was a different story. The dream season was a definite reality. Two weeks remained before the Bulldogs would play LSU, the Western Division champs, in the Georgia Dome for the SEC Championship. He had to get his act together before the game.

The headache worsened; the right side of his head felt like it was in a vise and the continuous throb drove him to his knees. He went to the kitchen for an ice pack from the freezer. His mom always kept them at the ready and had done so since he was eleven years old. He refused to take prescription medication for the headache and smiled at the irony, since he was pretending to be a druggie.

Leaving the kitchen, he noticed the door to the garage was ajar. A quick look revealed the garage door down and only his mother's car in the garage. He had not heard his father leave, but sudden returns to the hospital were commonplace in the medical field.

He started upstairs but saw that the door to his father's study was open. His father must have been in a hurry since he rarely left the door open and lately had locked it whenever he was not in the study.

Joshua eased open the door, concerned that someone might be present. He closed the door behind him, walked to the desk and sat in the plush leather chair. Holding the ice pack to his head with his right hand, he used his left to search the papers on the desk. Unsure what he was looking for, he searched for anything that would give him additional information about the mysterious import business.

His search revealed little of importance—just a few bills due for household expenses. It appeared his father was behind on some of the payments, understandable since his mother usually had taken care of those bills.

He retrieved a discarded newspaper from the wastebasket, placing the ice pack on it to prevent damage to the desktop. With his right hand free, he opened the top drawer of the desk. There were several envelopes in the drawer but all pertained to office business. He closed the drawer and rummaged through the middle and bottom drawers. Again he found nothing of importance, so he checked the pencil drawer under the desk top. There were paper clips, rubber bands, pencils and pens and a few handwritten reminders of items to be purchased at the grocery store but no information worth noting.

In frustration he slammed his hand on the desk, knocking the ice pack and the newspaper to the floor. He leaned over to pick them up and noticed a small piece of masking tape hanging from the bottom of the drawer. He got on all fours for a closer inspection and discovered a key held in place by the tape. He peeled the tape away and removed the key. None of the drawers on the desk had locks so he turned his attention to the walnut shelves along the wall. The long open shelves held medical textbooks and beneath them were built-in cabinets but, again, none were fitted with a lock.

He pushed back from the desk and moved closer to the cabinets. He opened the first, locating the wet bar. The mirror back reflected the labels of Maker's Mark, Glenfiddich Single Malt and Grey Goose Vodka. On the other side of the shelf was a box of Cuban cigars. His father apparently had some good contacts in the import business.

He closed the cabinet door and opened the second; a bunch of papers wrapped with a large rubber band fell out. Removing the band he discovered a map of Georgia and some printed advertisements for quail hunting in South Georgia.

He returned the papers and opened the third cabinet. Inside, he found a steel container, built in like a safe deposit box, with a single lock. The key fit. He turned it and pulled the door open, exposing a bonanza. He dropped to his knees by the cabinet door. *My God*, he thought, looking at four stacks of plastic-wrapped currency bundles and a .357 Magnum adjacent to them.

He removed one of the bundles, noting it was about an inch thick and contained one-hundred-dollar bills. He ran his fingers over the stacks and counted fifty packets. Each packet had a sticker attached in the upper right corner with the figure of ten thousand printed in ink.

A half million dollars. Why would Dad have that much money at home? Why did he have that much cash, period?

Joshua felt sick to his stomach over thoughts coursing through his brain. The money certainly explained the presence of the gun. Beneath the pistol was a heavy ledger, the type used by accountants.

He removed the pistol and placed it on the carpeted floor. He grabbed the edge of the ledger, slid it out, and while sitting on the floor with his back against the cabinet, he opened it.

The front page contained the heading of Ortega Import, the same company listed on the papers in the file boxes found earlier. The second page contained names of individuals and addresses, many of them in Atlanta, but several names were Spanish with addresses in Colombia, South America.

Joshua felt a large lump in his throat and he swallowed several times to calm himself. He had found the reason for his father's distraction. Subsequent pages listed delivery dates and quantities of cocaine, marijuana and heroin shipped from Colombia. Beneath several of the dates was the name "Manuel," but most recently, "Weber."

There was no doubt; his own father was the MAN.

Joshua's hands shook so badly, he almost dropped the book. He put everything back into the inner cabinet, locked it and closed the cabinet door. Returning to the desk, he taped the key back in place and left the study.

He would not go to the police with the information until he talked with his father, who was likely involved in PJ's disappearance. Laying everything on the line with him might be the way to get PJ back home—alive.

CHAPTER 41

On the drive home from the cabin, Smith was in torment, trying to solve the puzzle of Joshua's involvement. He wanted to believe PJ, but could he ignore the information that Pete had learned from that kid, Eddie? How could Joshua know? If he did, why hadn't he confronted his father?

Smith was so caught up in the dilemma, he was startled when he saw the marker at the entrance to Clarke County. He decided to assume Joshua knew nothing and, unless asked pointed questions, he would continue his normal daily routine.

When he entered the oak-lined street near his house, he searched the driveway for Joshua's Jeep. He didn't see it and somewhat relieved he drove into the driveway, clicked the remote and entered the garage. He listened to the purr of the powerful Mercedes engine for several minutes before he switched it off. Leaning back into the rich leather seat, he attempted to collect his thoughts.

Somewhere in the back of his mind, he heard the garage door thump as it met the concrete surface—something he rarely noticed. His brain filtered out the usual sounds and he became aware of others, out of place. He straightened up in his seat, looking around, searching for the source of the foreign noise. His hands were sweaty and he could feel the hard beat of his heart in his neck and head. The increased stress level was getting to him.

When he got the present mess cleared up, he was getting out of the business. Getting out of the business—getting out—a problem. They might not let him out. From deep within his brain, memory long suppressed became vivid again and he heard the horrific sounds from the pen in Colombia.

He entered the house, grabbed a glass, filled it with ice from the ice maker and went straight to his study. He needed quiet time so he turned off his pager from the answering service. He opened the cabinet door to the wet bar and removed the bottle of Glenfiddich Single Malt. After pouring two fingers of the brown liquid in the glass, he replaced the bottle on the shelf. He changed his mind again and took the bottle with him to his desk.

He sprawled out in his chair, propped his feet up on his desk and let the oversized leather chair envelop him like a faithful lover. He raised the glass to his lips, savoring the burn of the smooth liquor as it trickled down his throat. He closed his eyes and let the scotch do its work. He finished the remainder in the glass with his eyes still closed and soon felt the pressure leave his chest and his pulse rate drop.

Reaching for the bottle to refill his glass, he glanced down and saw an object on the floor, just beneath the edge of his desk. He brought the chair upright, leaned over and picked up a reusable ice pack, now a squishy jelly in a plastic bag. The sports page he had read the night before was damp and lying on the floor. His moment of contentment disappeared. Someone had been in the study since he left that morning.

His pulse raced as he yanked out the shallow desk drawer, retrieving the key from underneath. He went to the cabinet under the book case and relief swept over him when he saw the contents undisturbed. His hands shook as he opened the steel cabinet within. Things looked in their normal place, the money neatly stacked. His gaze locked on the ledger. It was placed with the binding to the right, opposite to the way he always placed it in the cabinet. He removed the ledger, flipping through the pages. Everything appeared to be present, but it did little to relieve his anxiety.

He was certain Joshua was the person who had invaded his privacy. Joshua had pieced together the puzzle and knew of the drug trafficking and would surmise his role in PJ's disappearance. He was glad he kept PJ alive. She was his bargaining chip. With her life in his control, Joshua would not involve the police. It was time for a father-son talk.

Joshua drove into his neighborhood, a picture of serenity. The wealthy Athenians who had called the Smith family neighbors and friends for years would be shocked beyond belief when they learned that one of their own, their doctor and friend, was a kingpin in the drug trade. Their sense of security would be shattered.

Different scenarios raced through Joshua's mind as he considered the most effective way to approach his father. He was convinced his father was involved in PJ's absence; threats of exposure wouldn't work. He needed to deal for her safe return, if she was still alive. His throat tightened at the thought.

He parked in the circular drive, entering the house through the front door; there was no longer a need for stealth. He saw his father's keys on the wooden key-holder in the kitchen but he checked the garage anyway. The Mercedes was there. Taking a deep breath to steel his nerves, he walked to the study. He knocked, expecting to be turned away and was surprised by the pleasant response.

"Come in, Joshua."

He pushed the study door open and peered inside, not sure what to expect. Maybe a gun pointed at his head or maybe some thugs lying in wait to beat him to death. Instead, he saw his father at his desk, his feet propped up, sipping an evening drink.

Joshua closed the door behind him. "How did you know it was me?"

"Your mother hasn't been in this study in months and seldom comes downstairs, so who else could it be? I knew it was only a matter of time until you came looking for me. You've been a busy boy, Joshua, and in much more than football."

Joshua's face reddened with anger, his father's flippant remark burning him like molten lead. "I'm not the only one who's been busy, you bastard. What have you done with PJ? If you've hurt her, I'll rip your rotten heart out with my bare hands." He moved toward the desk.

Smith stood, leaning forward with his hands on his desk. His mouth twisted into an evil grin. "Keep your distance, boy. I'm holding all the chips and you'll do what I say, if you ever want to see that little tart again."

Joshua no longer saw his father in front of him—now it was the MAN. The one he despised, the target of his search for the past months.

"What has PJ ever done to you? I know you have her somewhere—why did you take her?"

Smith kept the desk between him and Joshua. "Let's just say she was at the wrong place at the wrong time. I assure you she's safe where she is, and she'll remain that way if you do what I tell you."

Joshua felt sick to his stomach that he had ever loved this man. "I can't believe what you have done to yourself and this family. How can you live with the knowledge that you were responsible for Timmy's death? And, for God's sake, look what you've done to Mom."

"Don't you dare lecture me." His father's voice was cold, his face hard. "You've had it good your whole life. You've never known what it's like to be poor. You've never experienced working as a janitor in the same dorm where your college classmates lived. You've never heard the snickers of others when they made fun of your ragged and out-of-style clothes. You've lived the life of the blessed. You are a jock, worshipped by kids and adults alike. You drive nice cars and wear stylish clothes." Smith laughed suddenly.

"Did you think all the things I've provided for you and this family came from my medical practice? What a fucking joke! It took the government forty years but they accomplished their goal. Physicians are the patsies of the government and insurance companies. We do the hard work and accept the pittance they offer as payment for our services.

"All those years of doing without, while I was in college and medical school and residency, all wasted—so a bunch of politicians can give tax money away in exchange for votes, to make sure they get re-elected. Goddamn them. I hate them all. So I found another way to get the things I've earned and I don't share it with our corrupt government."

Joshua stared at the person who raved on like a madman, so unlike the dedicated physician he once knew his father to be. "Why drugs? You always taught us the weak used drugs."

Smith stabbed his finger at Joshua to make his point. "Exactly. There's a lot of money in drugs because the weak and the ignorant will always provide a ready market for a way to escape their miserable lives."

Joshua closed his eyes, unable to look at the man in front of him. "It's not just the poor that use drugs. Look what happened to Timmy."

His father wrinkled his nose as if he smelled a bad odor. "Like it or not, your brother was a weakling. He always needed a crutch. He was never like us."

"You bastard, don't you dare lump me with you. I'm not like you at all."

"Don't be so damn pious. Weber told me about you and your army of brats. He's sure you killed Manuel and the others. I always knew you were tough, but I didn't think you had the balls to step outside the law."

Joshua took a step around the desk, causing his father to retreat. "Weber is a total dumb ass. I knew he couldn't be the brains behind all this, but I didn't know for sure until I found your accounting book. You are the one I've been after—the others were pawns, but just so you'll know, I didn't kill Manuel or any of the others. I wish I had, but someone did it for me."

"Well, here I am. You've found me out. Are you able to kill your own father? Would that satisfy the blood lust and revenge you've sought so hard? Would you risk losing PJ to kill me?"

Joshua shivered with the realization that his father had complete control over him. The hatred he felt for the MAN was not diminished just because it turned out to be his own father, but he could not jeopardize PJ. It might be too late, but his love for her was greater than his thirst for revenge. He looked down at the desk, avoiding his father's face.

"What do you want me to do?"

"Have you told anyone of what you learned about me?"

"No, I knew I would have to deal with you for PJ."

"Keep it that way," his father said. "Call off your friends. Tell them anything you want but make sure they stop. Weber and Pete have already killed one member of your group. I wasn't aware of it until after the fact."

The fire in Joshua's belly was momentarily restored. "I know about Eddie. We've already taken care of Pete, and Weber's next."

"No, you heard what I said. It stops if you ever want to see PJ again. I'll take you to PJ later, but first I want you to see your friends and tell them it's all over. Spend your time getting ready for the SEC Championship game."

Joshua couldn't respond and simply nodded his agreement. He turned to leave the study, stunned that his father thought him so naïve. He knew this man, someone he had once loved so dearly, was now insane and would not hesitate to kill him and PJ to protect his illicit business. Knowledge of his father's intentions was one thing; what to do about them was another.

CHAPTER 42

Anderson sat slumped down in an unmarked Ford Taurus parked in a driveway near the Smith home. His nonchalant posture belied his anxiety. All his fingernails were bitten to the quick and at the moment he was chewing on his right thumbnail. He mumbled to Billings who was dozing behind the steering wheel. "Something's going to happen tonight, I can feel it in my bones."

Billings reached over and jerked the thumb from Anderson's mouth. "Stop that, it's unsanitary."

Anderson reacted by placing both hands under his thighs. "I can't help it. I refuse to start back smoking and I've chewed gum until my jaws are locked down. I picked a bad time to try to kick the habit."

"How many times I got to tell you? It ain't a habit. It's an addiction, just like these dope heads that pop pills, snort coke and smoke crack. Only difference is the poison you use is legal."

"Lighten up. Don't liken me to those scumbags. To change the subject, you know it's a reach to suspect Smith is involved in the girl's disappearance. Sergeant Askew told me Mrs. Smith stated her son wasn't at home when the girl visited."

"Think about what you just said," Billings replied. "How reliable is her information? The poor woman looks like she's gone around the bend."

The two detectives were silent for a while, each deep in thought over the present assignment.

Anderson broke the silence. "Hard to believe Joshua Smith would off his girl friend even if she discovered he was involved in drug trafficking."

"I agree with you but people do strange things when cornered. Maybe it was one of those knee-jerk reactions and he didn't intend to kill her."

They fell silent again. Anderson thought about the "hands off" warning they had received from Chief McElroy regarding Dr. Smith. The chief approved the double tail on Joshua but made it clear Dr. Smith was not to be questioned or harassed in any manner.

"McElroy is sticking his neck out on this assignment. If we blow it, we'll be riding one of those scooters downtown, writing parking tickets."

Anderson laughed so hard at his own joke, tears came to his eyes. "They would call us the 'meter misters.'"

Billings didn't see the humor. "Better than being called unemployed. We've got to make a score soon. The chief can only take so much heat from the commissioners before he starts causing some pain in our pockets."

Anderson nodded. "I think Carlos will come through on this tip. If he's right, the jock will lead us to something that might break this case wide open. Hell, all we need is a little opening. We can widen it ourselves."

Billings grabbed the steering wheel and, using it as leverage, repositioned his large frame. "I got you. It's like one of those jigsaw puzzles. Get the border done and the rest of the pieces fall in place."

Anderson focused on the front of the Smith house, his thumb going back to his mouth. "You know, I hope I'm wrong about Joshua Smith. He's got such great potential and would be a superstar in the pros. We're putting him at risk with the NCAA just by investigating him. I'm surprised the media hasn't picked up on our suspicions and started hounding the coaches and the athletic department."

Billings shifted his weight again. "The chief put a serious gag order on the entire department. Dr. Smith is a major citizen and false allegations against his son would bring down the whole department."

Their attention was diverted when they saw the front door of the Smith house open. Joshua walked out, pulled the door closed and walked to his Jeep.

Anderson picked up the radio handset and alerted the second team parked a block away north of the house. "Sixteen, this is Unit Twelve. Our target is leaving his house."

Billings waited until Joshua passed them driving toward the city before he started the engine and followed. He positioned their car several hundred feet behind the Jeep, maintaining the position for about a mile. When the Jeep made a turn onto a side road, they let Unit Sixteen pass them and pick up the tail. They continued to flip-flop for several minutes, puzzled at the circuitous route the Jeep was traveling.

"Do you think he's made us?" Billings asked.

"It sure looks like it. Where the hell is he going? We've traveled in a damn circle. We can't be more than two blocks west of his house."

Unit Sixteen passed them again, continued on Dogwood Trail and when the Jeep pulled over to the curb, they cruised past it.

"Unit Twelve. Sixteen here. Did you see what just happened?"

"Got you, Sixteen. We've turned into a driveway and have good cover. We'll maintain surveillance on the target. Stay on your present route until you are well out of sight, circle back to your original stake out point and remain there until you hear from us."

"Copy. Sixteen out."

Billings pounded his hands on the steering wheel. "What the hell is he doing?"

"Damn if I know. It looks like he's watching his own house. From his location he can see the driveway but can't be seen from his house. We'll play out this cat-and-mouse game and see what happens."

An hour passed before the scene changed. Billings was awakened from his brief nap by Anderson's voice. "Sixteen. Twelve. The Jeep is traveling in your direction."

"We see him. Doesn't the suspect's father drive a metallic silver Mercedes sedan?"

"That's affirmative."

"Well, it passed by us a few seconds ago and now the suspect is following it."

Anderson looked at Billings as they pulled out of the driveway to continue pursuit. "What the fuck is going on?"

The strange procession continued north from Athens on Highway 441 until it reached the intersection with Interstate 85. Anderson saw the red glow from the Jeep's brake lights when it turned onto the entrance ramp heading north on the interstate toward South Carolina.

"Damn partner. We have our gonads hanging out on this one. Don't know how much longer we can stretch this tail and still be legal."

Billings eased off the accelerator, allowing Unit Sixteen to take the lead. When the black Ford Explorer passed them he gave a half wave before answering Anderson.

"Wherever Smith stops, we'll call the local boys for help, but what are we going to do if he continues over the South Carolina state line?"

Anderson sighed. "I guess we'll pull off the road and stick our thumbs up our butts. No way can we call in the Carolina Troopers. What would we tell them? Let's just hope this train doesn't go that far."

"Got any thoughts of their destination?"

Anderson had pondered that same question for the past forty miles; he had no idea. "Maybe Dr. Smith has a boat on Lake Hartwell, but why would he go there this time of night and why is his son shadowing him?"

"Maybe he thinks his old man is seeing another woman and he's snooping around for his mom."

Anderson turned his head toward his partner to give him the full force of his raspberry. "Damn. You get crazier by the day. What a brilliant suggestion. If he wanted something on the side, surely he could find a willing partner closer to Athens. I've been in some strange cases before but this one tops them all. We have two government vehicles, four supposedly intelligent investigators traveling all over north Georgia and we have zilch to show for it. If we don't come up with something, the chief will roast our ass."

Joshua leaned forward, his chin almost resting on the steering wheel. The glare of oncoming headlights reflecting off the wet pavement distorted his vision and made the task of following his father more difficult. The windshield wipers were ineffective against the heavy downpour but he was able to keep the glowing taillights of his father's car in sight. He accelerated, closing the distance between the two vehicles. The storm made it hard for him to see but likewise prevented his father from recognizing he was being followed.

Joshua was so focused, he was unaware of the cars that had played leapfrog behind him since leaving Athens.

The rain eased and with the improved visibility, Joshua saw his father take the exit ramp to the Lavonia-Toccoa road. Joshua followed but slowed down when the Mercedes stopped at the top of the ramp. The big car turned onto the blacktop road, traveling two hundred feet before it pulled off into an Exxon station.

Joshua swung his Jeep in the opposite direction, entering the parking lot of a Wendy's restaurant. He drove around the building, stopping adjacent to several cars in the drive-through lane. From his vantage point, he watched the sedan. He could follow no matter which direction his father took when he left.

The radio crackled, startling Anderson. He grabbed the handset from the hook. "Twelve here."

"Twelve, we have just turned off at the Lavonia exit. We see the Mercedes at an Exxon station but can't locate the Jeep."

"Sixteen. Be careful you aren't spotted by the target. Drive into the opposite side of the station, if you can. Don't let the suspect's father see you or your license plate. Is he getting gas or taking a whiz?"

The crew of Unit Sixteen laughed. This tail was becoming comical. "He's getting gas."

Anderson ignored the laughter, but would attend to it later. "Pull around to the pumps on the other side and do the same. We're near the ramp. Is there another station nearby?"

"There's a BP station across the overpass."

"Good. We'll get gas there if we have time. Let us know which direction the Mercedes takes when it leaves the station. Do not follow until you see the suspect fall in behind the Mercedes. He's got to be somewhere nearby."

"Sixteen, out."

Joshua's wait was short. Within minutes the Mercedes passed by in the direction of Toccoa. He delayed for a few seconds, drove out of the parking lot and fell in behind his father. He prayed this chase would lead him to PJ.

Several minutes passed before Joshua once again saw the brake lights cast their reddish hue on the black asphalt. He slowed, anticipating another turn. The bright beam of light from the Mercedes revealed a narrow dirt road leading into a dense wooded area.

Now what? he thought. Follow the sedan down the dirt road and risk being discovered, or park his Jeep near the highway and advance on foot? He was unfamiliar with the area. He didn't know the length of the road or if there was another outlet. He decided to take his chances on foot.

He drove past where the sedan turned, parking his Jeep deep into some heavy brush. The area was desolate. When he switched off the headlights, he found himself enveloped by near total darkness. He remained seated, allowing his eyes to adjust to the dark. The night's silence was broken by popping sounds from the cooling engine.

From beneath the driver's seat he extracted a small flashlight. He removed the Glock from the glove compartment and with the gun in his jacket pocket and the flashlight in his left hand, he climbed out of the Jeep. He crept into the woods, parallel to the dirt road, but soon found it almost impossible to advance even with the flashlight. Better to travel on the road without the light, than stumble through the brush with a wavering light to announce his arrival.

Moving back to the road he crossed a small ditch and as he attempted to jump, his boot caught on a large rock at the edge of the road, throwing him to the ground. His head struck the ground hard and he swung wildly at imagined assailants.

Composing himself, he started down the road, waving his arms in front and using his feet to feel the slope of the road. He kept near the center of the road to prevent another fall. Staring into the black void, he saw a sudden flash of light ahead, to his right. He dropped to his knees, his eyes searching for the source of the light. He saw nothing nor heard a sound.

He moved back off the road into the trees. The undergrowth was less dense, allowing him to move with less noise in the direction of the previous flash of light. He paused after each step, listening for evidence of his discovery. His head throbbed from the fall and the intense effort of straining to see in the darkness. A beam of moonlight appeared, peeping through the storm clouds.

He covered ten yards with ease before the ground beneath his left foot gave way. He reached out blindly, grabbing a small shrub that prevented him from tumbling into a ravine. He got down on all fours, inching his way forward. At the bottom of the deep crevice was a stream swollen by the recent rains. He crossed it, crawling up the opposite side at an agonizingly slow pace, gauging the sturdiness of each handhold before he advanced. Finally he reached the top. Exhausted, he lay still for several minutes, holding his head between his arms, recognizing the onset of another migraine headache.

"Please God, not now," he whispered. He saw a shower of bright lights flickering behind his tightly closed eyes. His stomach contracted as he fought back a wave of nausea. He curled in a ball on the ground, his brain awash in a sea of pain.

Somehow voices penetrated the barrier and he got up, ignoring the headache. The voices carried well through the woods but not well enough for him to decipher the words. He was able to determine the direction, and he crawled toward the sound, sweeping his hands on the ground to avoid another fall.

The wind shifted and the voices became louder. Joshua froze in position. There were two voices and the owners were arguing loudly.

"I'm telling you, let me take her to the dam, wrap her in chains and sink her."

Joshua clinched his fists, realizing the person was referring to PJ. He heard his father's voice responding.

"Don't be so eager to be rid of her, Weber. Things have changed. My son has evidence implicating me."

Weber exploded, "How the hell did he find out?"

"Never mind how he found out. He hasn't gone to the police since he's up to his neck in trouble as well. He's not an idiot. He suspects we have his girl. We need her now more than ever. We can use her to get him to back off."

"This is fucking nuts, boss. We keep her out here much longer and someone is going to discover her. That would lead to sinking a bunch of bodies."

"In the long run, I don't care how many bodies you sink, but for now, she is not to be harmed. I'm not stupid. Joshua won't let it go that easy. Even if he did, we still would have to worry about the little bitch. We need her to bait Joshua. If I can get him out here, you can take care of both of them."

"You ... you want me to waste your own son?"

"Do I have a choice? Sorry, but I don't relish the idea of prison and being butt-fucked for the rest of my life by some perverted prick. If Joshua and the girl are even remote threats, they get eliminated."

"Man, you are one cold-hearted dude." Weber's voice sounded admiring.

"Never mind what I am. Just make sure you are here tomorrow and I'll get Joshua here. If things go well, we won't have to worry for a while. We'll close the operation down while the investigation goes on for Joshua's disappearance. His loss will create quite a stir in the sports world. I'll have to play the grieving father. You can head out for the Bahamas or wherever. I'll see that you have enough money to live well."

"What about you? Where are you going?"

"I've made plans but I can't go anywhere yet. I've still got to deal with Atlanta. I'd rather have the feds after me than Ortega."

One of the men moved and Joshua saw a sliver of light escape from a partially opened door. His blood ran cold at the callousness of his father's words. He shifted his weight to his left knee, so he could move his right leg forward. He stopped. The sliver of light became a bright opening. The men had entered what appeared to be a small cabin.

The light disappeared again and Joshua advanced, less concerned about noise. It appeared no one was outside the cabin. He climbed over a row of small shrubs, through a narrow grassy area and reached the side of the building. He crept around the wooden structure searching for a window or a back door. He made his way to the back where he saw shimmering moonlight reflecting off a body of water.

He stood, easing along the wall. His hands struck a window frame but no light escaped from within the cabin. Cautiously, he leaned against the window, placing his ear against the pane of glass. He heard his father's voice.

"I don't want to hurt you, PJ. I need to know how much Joshua has told you and if anyone else is involved."

PJ's voice quivered. "I told you and that other man, Joshua told me nothing."

The sound of a slap startled Joshua. His jaws tightened when he heard PJ cry out and he fought back the urge to bang on the window.

"Listen to me. Joshua has no idea what he's done. There are powerful people involved who won't hesitate a second to kill him and the rest of us. I've got to stop him before it gets to that point. Talk if you want to save him."

PJ spoke between sobs. "I don't know anything. I was in your office using the bathroom while I was waiting for Joshua. Connie told me it was okay."

Smith struck her again. "You lying tart. You were spying for Joshua, weren't you? My stupid wife let you in my office and I caught you."

Joshua heard PJ weeping and had to stop himself from charging into the cabin. He should have called Anderson. The detective had offered help but he had been reluctant to bring down his father. He'd foolishly thought his father had inadvertently become involved. Now he knew him for the monster he was.

Smith spoke again, almost pleading. "This is your last chance. I can't stay here all night and if you don't tell me right this minute, I'll call Weber back inside and let him deal with you for the rest of the night. His methods are crude but effective."

Joshua froze. Weber was outside. The night seemed colder, his senses heightened. He dropped to the ground, flattening against the wall. He listened for footsteps, half expecting Weber to walk up behind him and crush his skull. The wind whistling through the tall pines was the single sound he heard. A scent of tobacco smoke passed by in the breeze and he relaxed. Weber was out front smoking, waiting to be called back inside. Joshua resumed his position against the window and heard his father call out.

"Get in here, Weber."

Joshua heard the door open and close, and then boots scuffing across the floor.

"Has she talked?"

Smith replied in disgust, "No, but she will when I bring Joshua up here tomorrow. When they are forced to watch each other being tortured, they will tell us everything we need to know."

There was silence for several seconds before Weber spoke. "Is it okay if I have some fun with her tonight? I get bored."

"I don't care what you do with her after Joshua tells me what I need to know, but for now, leave her alone. When the time comes, you can have fun with her and make Joshua watch."

"No problem, boss. I never want you pissed at me. You are one bad dude."

"Sometimes life makes us that way. I've got to return to the hospital. Remember my instructions."

A murderous rage coursed through Joshua's body. At that moment, he could kill his father with his bare hands. He moved toward the corner of the building, his fingers gripping the butt of the gun in his jacket pocket. His mind no longer accepted the man as his father. He was someone who had ordered Weber to rape PJ and kill his own son.

Fury drove him along the edge of the wall to the cabin door. With no plan of action other than stopping the two men inside, he burst through the door, the gun an extension of his arm. His eyes fell on PJ, bound to a chair, her legs and arms wrapped with duct tape.

His momentary distraction gave Weber time to grab his gun from the dresser top. He fired off balance but the bullet caught Joshua in the upper part of his right arm making him drop his gun.

Weber grinned. "Looks like we don't have to wait until tomorrow."

Smith braced against the back wall, staring at his son. He walked over to Joshua and performed a cursory examination of his arm.

"There's no apparent bone or vessel damage. You'll be okay."

Joshua yelled at him, "Liar, I heard what you told Weber. You will kill me just as surely as you killed Timmy. Your fucking greed is phenomenal."

Smith appeared shaken, but he quickly recovered. There was blood on his hands from Joshua's wound. He wiped it away with his handkerchief and turned to Weber, who was pointing his gun at Joshua's head. "I don't think Joshua is in a cooperative mood. Tie him in a chair. Don't waste time or effort torturing him. Work on the girl. I'll be here tomorrow by noon."

CHAPTER 43

Anderson whispered into his handset for Maxwell and Buice, the officers from Unit Sixteen, to move closer to the cabin. Both units had failed to see the Jeep when they first passed but on circling back they spotted it parked in the brush. They left their cars and maneuvered their way down the narrow dirt road. They were within fifty feet of the cabin when they heard the gunshot.

Billings whispered to Anderson. "I'm going back to the car. I'll contact the Stephens County Sheriff's office for backup."

"Stay with the car until they arrive. Unless we hear more shots, we'll remain in position until we have more help."

Anderson crawled over to Maxwell and Buice and positioned them on the right side of the cabin. He started back to his original position but saw the cabin door open so he stopped. Smith stood in the doorway, silhouetted by the light from the interior. He conversed with someone, closed the door and walked to the Mercedes.

Anderson hugged the ground, bringing the handset up to his mouth. "Marvin."

"Got you, partner."

"The driver of the Mercedes is identified as Dr. Smith and he is leaving the area. Unknown numbers are inside, with Joshua Smith and possibly the girl. I can't leave this position. When Dr. Smith comes out, follow him."

There was no reply. Anderson heard heavy breathing. "Marvin, you okay?"

There was a brief pause before an answer came. "I'm okay, just out of breath. I ran to the car. Nothing I can do about Unit Sixteen's car but I'm out of sight and can fall in behind Smith when he leaves. I'll contact Stephens County right now."

"Don't tail him too close. He's on his way back to Athens. If you lose him, go to his house and make sure he doesn't leave. Call in backup in necessary."

Billings answered with a couple of clicks followed by a sarcastic, "Yes, mother."

CHAPTER 44

It was time for fun. Weber grabbed PJ's chair, dragging it in front of Joshua.

Joshua struggled against his bonds, his huge biceps bulging but he accomplished nothing except increasing his frustration.

Weber played with PJ's earlobes, smiling all the time at Joshua. He ran his tongue deep into her ears, his drool dripping onto her neck, which he licked with long deliberate strokes. He clamped his large hands over her ears to stop her from jerking her head. When she resisted, he slapped her hard and PJ, stunned, remained still, unable to prevent him from running his tongue over her lips.

He kissed her, sticking his tongue deep into her mouth. He jumped back, blood pouring from his lower lip. "You fucking slut. You bit me. I'll teach you to be nice to me. Soon you'll beg to suck my dick."

Weber stuck his automatic in the waistband of his pants. He unbuttoned the top of PJ's blouse, became impatient and ripped open the front. He retrieved a Buck knife from the back pocket of his jeans. Exposing the razor sharp blade, he waved it in front of her face before pressing it to the soft flesh under her chin. He turned his head toward Joshua, watching his reaction as he pulled the blade across PJ's neck leaving a thin streak of blood.

"Bite this, bitch, and I'll cut out your tongue."

Joshua bounced in his chair, his head shaking in rage.

Weber responded by snatching the duct tape from Joshua's mouth. "Got something to say, big football hero?"

"Leave her alone, you sick bastard."

Weber grinned. He liked this game; time would pass much faster. "If I don't, what the hell are you going to do?"

Joshua's took a deep, rasping breath and looked into Weber's eyes. "If you hurt her, I won't tell my father a damn thing no matter what you do to either of us. He'll have you butchered if you screw up his plans."

"Your old man doesn't have the balls. He acts tough when he's got me to do the hard stuff for him."

With a deliberate move, Weber dragged the knife edge from PJ's chin down between her breasts that heaved with each breath. He hooked the blade beneath the plastic clasp of her bra and with a flick of his wrist freed the full white mounds held captive by the lingerie.

PJ gasped in terror and squeezed her eyes shut.

"Leave her alone, you fucking maniac," Joshua shouted.

Weber spun, the steel flashed, leaving a bloody slash across Joshua's left cheek. "Watch your fucking language in front of the lady."

Weber doubled over in laughter at his macabre humor. He folded the knife, returning it to his back pocket. He moved behind PJ and began massaging her shoulders. With a quick move, he grasped the collar of her blouse, yanking it down to expose her upper torso. The duct tape wrapped around her arms prevented the blouse from coming off completely.

Joshua made eye contact with PJ, willing her to focus on him. He loved her, but until this moment, he never knew the depth that love went. Tears of anguish filled his eyes but he blinked them away when he saw PJ's lips form a trembling smile. She understood his love, he thought.

Weber, unaware of the silent signals, slid his hands down onto the girl's breasts, cupping them in his hands. He tweaked her nipples, rolling them between his thumbs and index fingers, achieving a false signal of desire when they became erect.

"Hey, look here, big jock, your lady is a slut. She wants a real man and I have just what she needs."

Weber moved around in front of PJ, leaning over her as he forced his hand down the front of her sweat pants. He rammed his fingers between her legs, causing her to cry out.

Joshua could take no more. He rocked the chair forward, rising up on his toes, and with all his strength launched himself at Weber. His head caught Weber in the face.

Weber staggered back from the blow, blood streaming from a cut over his right eyebrow. He pulled the gun from his waistband and fired wildly, the bullet slamming into the heavy front door.

Anderson was at the back of the cabin just below the covered window. He heard the commotion inside, the gunshot, followed by a crashing sound and more gunfire. He spoke into his handset but didn't receive a reply. Fearing the worst, he ran to the front of the building. The men of Unit Sixteen had torn the door from its hinges.

Anderson raced past the destroyed door, crashing over Buice, who was on the floor. Maxwell was sprawled against the wall, his massive hands trying to stem the blood flowing from his gut. Anderson rolled to his left away from the door, colliding with the up-ended chair to which Joshua was tied.

Joshua screamed a warning to Anderson. "Watch out. Weber's behind the kitchen counter."

Anderson crawled toward the counter that split the back portion of the room. Just as he got to PJ, he saw movement as Weber came around the end of the counter, firing at almost point-blank range. Anderson grabbed PJ's chair, pushed it over, and covered it with his body. He brought his weapon around and got off a single shot before he was struck twice in the chest. He toppled over, his weapon sliding from his hand.

Weber moved like a cat across the blood-slicked floor, retrieving Anderson's gun while casting a glance toward Maxwell, recognizing that he was no longer a threat. He backed away from the others and stood alongside the counter.

"This shit has gotten out of hand. I'm not waiting on Smith or anyone else. I'm going to finish off the whole bunch of you."

He pocketed his automatic and hefted Anderson's gun. "Some shit, huh, getting wasted by your own gun." He aimed at Anderson's head. In the corner of his vision he saw movement in the doorway.

He spun toward the door in time to see a slight figure fire both barrels of a twelve-gauge shotgun. The deer slugs tore into his chest, blowing apart his heart and lungs.

The hooded man paused in the doorway, looked about the room and started to enter, but stopped when ear-piercing sirens approached the cabin. He turned his attention back to the occupants of the cabin. Holding the Mossberg in his gloved left hand, he fished a switchblade from his back pocket and moved toward Joshua.

PJ whimpered when she saw the knife and the hooded figure moving toward Joshua. She cried out, "Please don't hurt him."

The blade cut through the duct tape on Joshua's arms like slicing through water. The figure reversed the knife, handing it to Joshua, handle first. He squeezed Joshua's arm. "For Timmy and Eddie," he said, and he vanished into the night.

Joshua cut away the rest of the tape, freeing his legs and moved to Anderson's side. Ignoring the burning pain in his arm, he rolled the detective on his back and opened his jacket. The front of Anderson's shirt was saturated with blood, mixed with bubbles that escaped around the holes in the shirt.

A whistling sound escaped from under Anderson's shirt and Joshua remembered sometime in the past his father talking about a patient with a sucking chest wound. Joshua pulled the remaining pieces of the duct tape from his arms and placed several patches of the tape on Anderson's chest. The musical sounds ended but the rhythmic breathing became shallow, replaced by intermittent gasps.

"No," Joshua screamed.

He placed his fingers on the side of Anderson's neck. The carotid pulse was weak. Placing his hand under the wounded man's neck, Joshua tilted the head back and placed his lips over Anderson's mouth. He blew hard, feeling the resistance from the collapsed lungs.

"Oh God. I'm losing him. He grabbed the knife and crawled to PJ's side. He freed her bound arms and legs and pleaded, "Please help me."

The two of them positioned themselves on each side of Anderson. They began the coordinated efforts of mouth-to-mouth and chest compressions.

CHAPTER 45

The Mercedes sedan with its sole occupant rocketed toward Athens. Smith kept his eyes focused on the highway but his mind was elsewhere, thoughts racing through his head. He drove through the small town of Arcade at eighty miles per hour. Realizing what he had done, he stole a glance in the rear-view mirror to make sure cops were not on his tail. His pounding heart convinced him it was time to cut and run.

There was no time to consider Weber, Joshua, PJ or Constance. It was time to grab his stash and get out of the country. With his false passports he could fly to the Cayman Islands and access his accounts there. He would move them to Switzerland, and settle somewhere in Europe. All his accounts wouldn't total what he had planned but it would allow him to live very well for the rest of his life. He wasn't worried about Interpol, but the thought of Ortega chilled his soul.

He drove into the garage, feeling secure when the door closed behind him. He took a deep breath and slumped down in the driver's seat. For a moment he sat there, visualizing his plans. He had an overnight bag packed and ready in his study. It would take just a few minutes to pack the currency and bonds in a duffel bag, and the clothes he wore, though wrinkled, were presentable enough to take a Caribbean flight. Anything else he needed he could pick up in the Caymans.

Billings slowed his vehicle when he approached the Smith house. He saw two black-and-whites parked within a block of the house and he murmured his thanks for his police brothers who answered his call. Following his instructions they were out of sight of the house.

He parked near the car to the north of the house. Approaching the vehicle, he flashed his badge. "Thanks, fellows, for getting here so quick. Is he already inside?"

"Yes, sir," the driver said. "He pulled into the garage and closed the door about ten minutes ago. My partner is around back covering the back exit."

"Good job. Radio the men in the other unit to join your partner in the back. I want you to find concealment closer to the front entrance. I'm going in through the service door next to the garage."

"What are your orders if Dr. Smith comes out the front door?"

"That won't happen. He'll need his vehicle, but if he does, consider him armed and dangerous."

Smith placed the overnight bag and the locked duffel bag at the top of the concrete steps leading to the garage. He left the door open, the light from the kitchen illuminating the dark interior of the garage. He opened the passenger's door, folded his jacket and laid it across the seat. He popped the trunk, returned to the steps and, smiling with satisfaction at the weight of the duffel bag, he placed it in the trunk along with his overnight bag. He closed the trunk and made his way around to the driver's door.

He looked up in surprise at the thin figure standing at the front of his car holding his automatic shotgun. "What are you doing here?"

Constance's face resembled one that could be on the cover of a Stephen King novel. "Did you think me a total fool? I figured out what you've been doing and I know you killed Timmy and you've probably killed Joshua and PJ. Do you think you can just run away and hide?"

Smith remained at the open door to his car. He didn't have a weapon, nor did he think he needed one. "I have to say, you surprise me," he said. "I haven't given you enough credit for your savvy. We can discuss that at another time. I must be going."

He made a half turn toward the interior of the car. The first blast tore through the car window, sending chunks of glass and number four shot into his face and neck. He staggered away from the car, fell to his knees and pulled himself upright by the bumper of the Lincoln. Using his sleeve to wipe blood from his eyes, he started toward Constance.

He accomplished four steps before the second shot ripped into his left knee, knocking him off his feet. He rolled over on his back, reaching up with his right hand to his wife who was standing over him.

She ignored the silent plea, placing the third shot in the center of her husband's chest, shredding his heart.

Billings tried the service door and finding it locked, turned toward the front entrance. He stopped when he heard voices in the garage. It was apparent at least two people were in there, but how many more, he couldn't tell. With hand signals he maneuvered the other officer to a position closer to the garage.

Billings moved against the door, placing his ear against the wooden surface. He jumped back when the first shot was fired. He pulled his weapon and, backing up a couple of feet, he threw all his weight against the door. It gave but remained closed. He plowed into it again at the same time he heard the second shot. The door crashed inward and Billings rolled against the wall. His eyes took in the unbelievable scene in a glance.

Before he could speak, the shotgun roared again. From his hiding place, he saw Constance Smith standing next to a tool cabinet, a smoking shotgun pointed at the floor.

"Freeze and drop your weapon."

The warning shout fell on deaf ears. The petite woman wearing a white robe splattered with blood dropped the shotgun on the floor and walked up the steps back into the house.

Billings crept low around the rear of the Mercedes and saw what remained of Dr. Smith sprawled on the floor in a pool of blood. With his Glock 40mm automatic at the ready, he entered the house through the kitchen and into the foyer. He saw Mrs. Smith just as she turned away from the top of the stairs. He waited for several seconds before following her up the stairs, the automatic extended in front of him with both hands.

He found her sitting in her deceased son's room, looking through the pages of a photo album. He holstered his weapon and started back downstairs.

EPILOGUE

The fluorescent lights overhead flickered when Anderson opened his eyes. The lights were just one of the many annoyances that were driving him crazy. The doctors had taken away his morphine drip so the naps were getting shorter and the time between oral pain medications longer.

"I've got to get out of here," he said to the apparently empty room.

The room at the Athens Regional Medical Center, however, was not empty. Billings dozed in a chair next to the bed and came awake when Anderson spoke. He yawned as he sat up from his slumped position.

"Believe me, partner. The nurses have already petitioned the doctors to discharge you as soon as possible. You are one royal pain in the ass to them."

Anderson attempted to laugh but stopped. The pain in his chest permitted only a chuckle. "How long you been here?"

"Which time? You've been lying around for six days. They wouldn't let me stay in ICU with you, but I've been in this chair since they moved you into this room. Not a bad room either. They must think you are some kind of hero. Shit, all you did was get your ass shot."

Billings rose from the chair, stretched, and pushed the bedside table over Anderson's bed. "This is your breakfast. It's cold, but I wouldn't let them wake you up when it came. Why the hell do they serve breakfast at six-thirty?" He moved to Anderson's side and helped him sit up in the bed.

"To piss me off," Anderson said.

The two men remained silent while Anderson pushed his eggs and bacon around on the plate. After eating a few bites he shoved the tray away. "I know about Buice. How's Eileen doing?"

"Okay, what you'd expect from a former Marine's wife. She spends a lot of time with Barbara Maxwell at the hospital. Maxwell is better but will be crapping in a baggie for the rest of his life. They took out half his gut. Still, that's better than Buice. Poor guy was dead before he hit the floor. The medical examiner said the bullet hit dead center of his heart."

Anderson turned his head away, trying to compose himself. He fretted more over the loss of Buice than he did over his own near-death experience. He turned back to Billings. "What about the kids?"

"If you're referring to Joshua and PJ, I suggest we start calling them adults after what they endured. They're doing okay. He won't be able to play in the SEC Championship game. The muscles in his arm were torn up, nothing permanent, but he can't heal fast enough to play."

Anderson wasn't concerned about the game. "What's his legal status?"

A wide grin appeared on Billings' face. "No problem. The DA agreed there was no direct evidence linking him to the murders, and the drug purchases were classified as 'unofficial' undercover work. Really means the guys downtown didn't want the hometown boy dragged through the muck after what the media did to his father's name. He has decided to forego the pros and he plans to enter law school. He wants to continue his crusade against drug dealers but from the legal side. He and PJ plan to get married next summer and we both have invitations."

"What happened to Mrs. Smith?"

"She's in a private mental hospital. Joshua told me the prognosis is not good. The poor woman broke under the strain. She resides in her own world now. Joshua said she smiles all the time but never speaks. He thinks she's finally with Timmy."

Silence hung over the room. Billings walked to the end of the bed to see if Anderson had fallen asleep. He was startled when Anderson spoke.

"Who?"

Billings laughed. "Who? You become an owl?"

"You know what I mean, asshole. Who was our killer? More importantly, who was the mystery person who saved all our butts at the cabin?"

Billings stood at the window watching gray clouds rolling in from the west. There was a good chance the person was one and the same and wasn't experiencing the same weather.

"Doug, you damn near lost your life. Buice did lose his and other lives have been changed forever. Promise me when you get out of here, you will let this drop. The chief's happy, the media's happy and no one even remembers about the deaths of the dealers."

Anderson made no promise but instead responded with a sense of certainty in his voice. "It was Carlos. I believe he became an avenging angel because they killed Timmy Smith and tried to set him up to take the fall. He became a protector of Joshua, who foolishly thought he had the savvy to track down his brother's killer. Carlos isn't around anymore, is he?"

Billings plopped into the chair, afraid where this conversation was heading. "No, he hasn't been seen in weeks. I would imagine he returned to Mexico."

"He probably did," answered Anderson.

He rolled away from Billings, wearing a crooked smile, picturing the little Mexican in Memphis looking for Elvis.

An old truck with more rust spots than paint pulled off Highway 17 south into a motel parking lot and parked under a massive oak tree. An elderly gentleman was sitting in a rocker on the porch of the office. A large black cat reclined lazily in his lap. Doyle Strickland smiled when he saw his visitor.